THE FALCONERS

Fort Eden

STORY BY EDWIN MCRAE
WRITTEN BY CHRIS KLUWE

ACKNOWLEDGEMENTS

The Order of the Falconer would like to offer special thanks to the following Falconers.

Silvester Sang for his splendid Falconers portraiture.

Rachel Rees, our hawk-eyed editor-in-chief.

Kirawat Sahasewiyon for designing the Falconers titling.

Rusharil Hutangkabodee for forging the official Falconers badge.

Shane Rees for his consummate cover design.

Without their generosity and dedication, this fictional work would not have been possible.

1

Asylum

SALIVA-GLISTENING FANGS HISSED PAST Patricia's ducking head, and she rolled backwards with a curse, her hand dropping to her side. She spun up onto one knee, pistol barking gold-sheathed bullets, and the grotesquely bulging body of what was once a hunting hound crashed to the floor, grey film spreading across its lifeless eyes. Thick black blood spread from its distended muscles across the unfinished interior tiles of the Seacliff Asylum, and Patricia crawled up next to a wall, her hands already busy reloading.

One down, she thought. Of course, there's at least five more Thralls roaming around in here. And after seeing what they did to the village…

Unbidden, her thoughts returned to the gruesome scene that lay outside. The entire Seacliff village, eighteen families, many with children, rendered down into so many bloody lumps of meat. The most wretched scene, and one she knew would haunt her sleep for months to come, had been the village hall. Five strong men, builders working on the almost finished asylum, lying scattered in front of the hall's shattered wooden doors. Inside, a charnel house, limbs and indiscernible parts of human bodies so intermingled that she couldn't tell how many lay dead, and all about, the constant buzzing of flies driving her nearly to insanity.

Farlan's not due for another hour at least. Bloody hell.

Patricia peered around the corner, searching for signs of the other Cullers in the murky late-afternoon light drifting through the empty window frames and half-raised walls. Brief movement caught her eye and she raised her pistol to her ear. Before she could take aim, a tangled and gooey web shot past her face, hitting the wall with a wet splat. She pulled back and snarled, heart pounding in her chest.

That was a fucking spider. Three feet or more tall. Wish you'd show up early for once in your life, old man. I'm completely outgunned here.

Seconds passed like hours, the air heavy and still. Patricia risked another glance. She saw the Culler darting out a doorway, segmented legs churning like pistons, and sprang up after it, vaulting one of the unfinished walls in her haste. The doorway grew in front of her like a gaping mouth. At the last instant, she turned her run into a slide, woolen trousers gliding almost frictionless across the smooth tiles. The doorway passed overhead and a jagged chitin leg scythed across where her midsection would have been had she remained upright. Patricia coolly emptied six bullets into the red and white abdomen of the Culler, reducing it to arachnid pulp. More black blood spattered down onto the once pristine tiles.

Eerie howls and yips filled the room, a grim cacophony of chaos. Another gruesomely warped hound padded into the asylum, followed by the elongated shape of a mastiff, grown to near three times its normal length, looking almost like a fur covered komodo dragon. Saliva dripped from two sets of jaws as her enemies split apart to flank her, their movements coordinated with unsettling intelligence.

Two against one, eh? Farlan said Davie Worthington took on two Hunters once. Took them a week to find all his bits for burial.

Patricia shouted, burying her emotions in the primal sound, and charged to her right, aiming for the mastiff. It flowed sinuously towards her, jaw distending impossibly wide. Behind her, Patricia heard the clattering scrabble of the hound's claws on tile. She dove left before the mastiff could snap its teeth shut on her, sliding once more across the floor. Her shoulder slammed into a wooden support beam, but her revolver was already spitting out bullets, the killing gold slamming home into the mastiff's exposed side.

It whined just once, a mewling, pitiable cry, then toppled over. Patricia had no time to savor her triumph. The shadow of the hound was in the air above her, descending fast.

2

Load of Bull

PATRICIA FORCED HER ACHING MUSCLES into motion, kicking up as hard as she could at the creature. Her boot connected with its right shoulder, shifting it just enough so its head slammed into the support beam right next to hers. The upper half of its body crashed into her, nearly crushing her ribcage. The smooth metal of her Falconer's badge dug into her chest and she felt a thin trickle of blood roll down her sternum. Dazed, the hound fell to its side, and Patricia whipped an arm around its neck, clinching herself against its back, and locking in a chokehold. Muscles tensed beneath her elbow, like coiled steel wires, and then the hound was kicking and writhing, spittle flying from its snapping fangs as they rolled across the floor.

Am I seriously trying to wrestle a Thrall right now? If I make it out of this alive, Farlan's going to laugh his arse off.

She tightened her arms, trying to choke the dog out, but it showed no sign of relenting. A paw caught her lower leg, gashing a shallow set of tracks along her calf. Patricia hissed in pain.

Shit. How am I going to kill this thing? Can't let go, and I still need to reload. Knife won't do anything, it's plain steel. The only gold I have is my Falconer's badge…

The hound twisted again, trying to break free, and Patricia wrapped her legs around its midsection, heedless of the raking claws tearing at her. Summoning every last ounce of strength, she heaved back, reaching her bracing arm under her shirt, and managed to close her hand around the smooth shape of her badge. The hound jerked forward, causing her to snap the leather thong from around her neck, but the swooping falcon remained in her grasp, its outstretched wings prickling her palm. With a grunt, she brought her hand to the hound's throat, and dragged those wingtips across the beast's fevered skin like a knife, splitting it open and spilling forth a torrent of black blood fecund with maggots. The hound kicked once and then fell still, seeming to deflate underneath her. Patricia scrambled to her feet, checking for signs of infestation on herself as she gasped for breath.

Two black maggots squirmed along her forearm and began to burrow into her flesh. Patricia grabbed her knife. Seconds later, two strips of her skin lay on the floor, and another pair of scars joined the trackwork already decorating her arms. She sank to the ground with a sigh, her entire body aching. A quick slash produced a strip of her shirt, and she began to wrap it into a makeshift bandage, dark red flowers blooming upon the fabric. Suddenly, a bellowing roar echoed from behind her and Patricia looked up with a curse.

A nightmare loomed over her, blood-matted hide and bone-yellow horns stretching nearly to the ceiling, eyes rolling in red-rimmed sockets.

Oh, come on. A bull? Two thousand bloody pounds of gods-be-damned bull?

Hands still as stone, she scrambled in her pocket for more bullets. Nothing met her questing fingers but sturdy woolen cloth. Her heart sank.

They must have fallen out when I was wrestling the other Thrall. Guess that's that, then.

The bull bellowed again, and Patricia bellowed back, one last act of defiance.

"Fuck off, you Culler bastard!"

The shotgun blast sounded like a cannon in the enclosed space, turning the bull's horned head into a fine black mist. Its body swayed for a second, then toppled to the floor with a resounding crash. Through the ringing in her ears, Patricia became aware of the sound of boot heels striking the floor. A grizzled figure in a dull red kilt stepped through the doorway, smoke wafting from the muzzle of his double barreled shotgun.

"You okay there, lass?"

She felt herself slump back in exhaustion and relief.

"Farlan. I thought you weren't going to make it."

Farlan lowered his shotgun and pulled out a flask, taking a long drink.

"Almost didn't. Lucky I saw that nasty gull thing circling over the village, so I thought I'd come investigate."

Patricia raised her head in alarm.

"There were five of them!"

"Easy lass, easy. That's one Culler that won't be flying again, I promise you that. Now, on your feet."

Groaning, Patricia hauled herself upright, and started gathering scattered bullets back into her pockets.

"What's the rush, old man?"

Farlan grinned, but there was no humor in it.

"This many Thralls this close to Fort Eden? If we don't get there soon, there won't be a Fort Eden to get to."

3

Warpers

Field Report to Falcon's Hall, Hamburg, Germany
Falconer Luc Barbier
October 5th, 1867
Port Fairweather, New Zealand

ENCOUNTERED A NEW SPECIES OF CULLER TODAY. I've decided to name the aforementioned beast a "Warper," owing to its habit of warping the body of its host into a form more suitable to the destruction of life and limb to those unfortunate enough to cross its path. The afflicted creature that led to this entry began its existence as a brushtail possum, genus *trichosurus vulpecula*, native to New South Wales, but this particular specimen bore as much relation to its common brethren as I do to a chimpanzee.

A normal possum that one would expect to encounter measures barely half a meter from tail to nose, but the animal I had the misfortune of meeting was near a meter long, and possessed of a tail resembling the jagged teeth of a hacksaw, its vertebrae twisted into razor sharp spines. The wretched beast

8

leapt down from an overhanging branch straight onto my unfortunate horse's neck, Esperer, a lovely natured chestnut mare. Before I could do so much as draw my pistol, the damned thing had opened her neck clear to the bone by wrapping its tail around her and constricting.

Thankfully, I had the good sense to leap from the saddle during poor Esperer's demise, else I fear I would have found myself pinned underneath her bulk and at the mercy of the enthralled possum's fifteen centimeter claws. It seems a common feature of the Warper is to enhance its host's natural defences, often to a level unimaginable by those unfamiliar with the Culler threat.

Mourning the loss of my faithful mare, I nonetheless utilized the years of Falconer training afforded to me. As the Warper leaped through the air towards my face, I emptied three gold slugs into the beast with my Chamelot-Delvigne pistol. Quite a jump it was, measuring near three full meters, and had I not fired and then ducked away, the twisted thing would have landed square upon my brow.

Once again I am compelled to ruminate on the peculiar qualities of the Warper Culler, specifically its ability to temporarily enhance the speed, strength and offensive capabilities of common animals. I say 'temporary,' as these 'enhancements' tend to put so much strain on an animal's physiology that they only live but a few months post-transfiguration. When their host is thus spent, the Warper Culler simply detaches itself from the carcass and goes in search of a new host. The discovery of this particular point of information cost me no small amount of money in rabbits. Please note the reimbursement form included in this envelope.

As far as anatomical structure goes, this nefarious little Culler has the dimensions and basic anatomy of an Ixodidae, a 'Hard Tick,' yet it differs from its mundane cousin in two quite remarkable ways, something I have discovered through a series of blood samples taken from 'Thralls,' the name I've given to the mammals, reptiles, and birds I've seen 'enthralled' by a Warper. These observations were garnered under carefully controlled laboratory conditions, of course.

Once the Warper punctures the skin of its victim and accesses the bloodstream, it then releases two chemicals that are quite diabolical in their utility. The first toxin takes control of the host's instincts so that the Warper may manipulate the enslaved animal's behaviours. It tends to favor territorial hostility, exacerbating aggression to quite disturbing levels. I suspect that it bears a similarity with the *toxoplasma gondii* that frequently affects mice, lessening their distrust of their feline predators.

The second toxin, if it can be believed, is even more nefarious than the first. It infiltrates the pituitary gland and activates bone and tissue growth in alarming proportions. Using the creature's own endocrine system, the Warper transfigures the animal in a similar way that a potter might mould clay. The results are both miraculous in nature, and hideous in design.

The most striking transfiguration I have thus far witnessed

is that of an Amazonian anaconda, turned quite literally into a multi-headed hydra that would have been far more at home in a Greek myth, each head capable of snapping at me independently. Thankfully, unlike its mythological counterpart, the creature's heads did not grow back after decapitation. By comparison, my initial encounter with the possum that slaughtered my poor Esperer might well seem pedestrian, and I fear for my fellow Falconers who might also encounter such gigantic abominations.

During my recent months in Port Fairweather, I have noted a marked increase in Warper numbers and activity. I have written to the Falconer way station in New South Wales, requesting reinforcements, but have as yet received no response.

If Warper numbers continue to increase, I believe it is a strong indication that the Fairweather settlement's expansion and resulting deforestation has not gone unnoticed. If this situation is not nipped in the bud, one way or another, New Zealand's capital might find itself in a troubling predicament.

May the Archives find this information useful,
Luc Barbier, Officer of the Order of the Falcon

4

Letters of Gold

TWO HORSES WALKED THROUGH THE NIGHT, thick fog muffling their plodding hoofsteps. A burly figure atop one of them shivered and pulled his leather coat tighter around his body. Soft tinkling echoed from his pockets. The tiny lantern attached to his saddle swayed then stilled, its circle of light revealing little more than a few feet ahead.

"This bloody fog cuts worse than any Culler claw, I'll tell you that true, lass. What'd you say this was called again in that language of yours?"

Patricia looked over at him, the tattoo on her chin glistening with the damp of the fog in the lamplight.

"We call it 'freezing ground fog,' Farlan. Like normal people."

"Well, can't argue with that. It's colder than a witch's tit." Farlan reached into his coat, producing a small flask, and tilted it into his mouth. "Ahhh, that's the stuff. Warms the body better than any fire on a cold night." He nudged his horse closer. "Patricia? Care for some?"

"No, thank you. I still don't understand how you haven't died of alcohol poisoning yet."

Farlan took another swig from the flask and tucked it back into his coat, then patted his stomach and winked.

"Deep, dark Falconer secret. Maybe I'll teach it to you someday. Of course, it would help if you were Scottish."

Patricia scowled.

"I have enough trouble being who I am already. Or did you already forget what happened last time we were here?"

Farlan laughed, a rolling avalanche of sound.

"Oh, lass, how could I forget? Breaking you out of Fort Eden Gaol remains one of the best memories of my life. You should have *seen* the expression on that warden's face when I blew out half his wall."

"I would prefer not to see any more wardens in my life, and speaking of which, aren't you the slightest bit worried that they'll arrest us on sight when we get into the city?"

Farlan's horse whickered as a deeper shadow appeared in the fog, gradually resolving into the splintering timbers of a rundown hovel, its wooden shutters tightly closed. Farlan reached down to give the mare a quick pat on the neck.

"Easy, Proof. Easy. No, lass, that was over five years ago. Means it never happened. Besides, you've got one of these, now."

Farlan tapped his thick shirt, underneath which lay a golden medallion in the shape of a swooping falcon, cool against his bare skin. More houses appeared in the looming darkness, breaching the frozen air like creatures surfacing from some chthonian abyss. Patricia reached up to her own shirt, feeling the forever attacking bird nestled atop her collarbone, its claws cleaned since Seacliff.

"Yes, that's comforting for you, Farlan. You're a white man. Of course they'll listen to you. I'm a half-breed, and a *woman*. You think a piece of gold is going to stop some gang of thugs wearing equally shiny badges?"

"You've got a pistol, too, right? What'd I teach you?"

Patricia's mouth unknotted into a sharp smile.

"Beat 'em over the head until they listen, and if they don't listen, shoot 'em and find someone who will."

"Aye, that's the one."

"I can't kill the whole city."

"No, but if there's a Culler in Fort Eden, it might kill the city for you. Seacliff was just the start. Our real work begins here."

Patricia's grin faded away at the reminder. There'd been a letter from Farlan's nephew, a constable in the Fort Eden police force. He'd talked of missing gold and peculiar happenstances. To a non-Falconer, merely another news item to ignore in a busy world, but to a Falconer...

Missing gold and peculiar happenstances were the calling cards of a Culler.

Farlan had contacted her a fortnight earlier, utilizing the 'newfangled' telegraph wires that seemed to be sprouting up everywhere, and Patricia knew at once they had to investigate.

A pack of Thralls in a remote hamlet was bad enough, but a Culler in the second-largest city in New Zealand? The death toll would be catastrophic. Fort Eden needed Falconers, and quickly.

Even if they did try to sentence you for murder last time you were here, she thought grimly.

5

Warm Welcome

MUD GAVE WAY TO PACKED DIRT, and even more houses appeared, many sharing walls. Soon, the two Falconers found themselves following the twisted maze of a street, wooden buildings rising up overhead like the sides of a narrow canyon. In the distance, a low howl echoed mournfully.

"You sure you know where you're going, Farlan?" Patricia asked, keeping her voice low.

"Of course. Into the city."

"That doesn't really sound like an answer."

"I've been operating in this area for years now, lass, and while it's not the easiest city to navigate, time brings some familiarity. The outer lanes are confusing, true, but eventually we'll find one of the big thoroughfares. Then it's just a matter of… hold up, lass, someone's coming. Let me do the talking."

Farlan flicked the safety off on his shotgun, the metal making a quiet *snikt*, and Patricia let her hand rest on the butt of her pistol, ready to draw in an instant if necessary. The sound of nailed boots clicked closer until a uniformed man stood in front of them, a rifle cradled in his arms, the tin star of the constabulary drooping from his chest.

"State your business!"

"Two travelers, looking for the harbor," Farlan answered in his gruff Scottish burr. "Any chance you can give us some directions?"

The man, his bearded face smudged with dirt, glared up at them, his eyes lingering on Patricia.

"These horses belong to you? You and your mongrel looking to make a quick escape after nicking some poor farmer's mounts?"

Patricia's hand tightened on her pistol, her knuckles as white as the mist. Farlan nudged his horse to put himself between her and the night watchman, his shotgun casually aimed just off-bore.

"Friend, it's a cold night, and we're simply looking to get where we're supposed to go."

"And what's your business at the harbor?" the watchman sneered.

"We're meeting a friend coming in on one of the clippers from Port Fairweather, and we'll be staying here for at least a couple days. So what say you let us be on our way and no one has to have their night made any more miserable than it already is."

The watchman scowled at Farlan, his fingers opening and closing on the stock of his rifle. Patricia tensed. Entering the city over the body of one of its policemen would no doubt hamper their efforts to investigate the Culler, but neither was she going to let some idiot with a gun threaten her and Farlan. If it came to it, she would shoot first and answer questions later. Besides, she was about 95% sure she could take out his gun without hurting him... too much.

Farlan, perhaps sensing her train of thought, spoke once more.

"Look, friend, the harbor can't be that far, right? Maybe what we need is to find you a nice alehouse near there, one that's warm and generous with a pour, and you can spend some time out of this miserable fog. On us," he finished, dipping two fingers into his belt pouch and flipping out a golden sovereign to the watchman.

The man snatched it out of the air, then bit down on it. Nodding his head, he tucked the coin away into a pocket, and let his rifle drop to point at the ground.

"Aye, it's too bloody cold out here anyway. Not that the bastards in charge care, it's not them freezing their arses off. Nice and warm in their new houses, sleeping the dreams of the rich, and I'm stuck out here in the muck. Like to see them do a night on the streets. Can't see a damn thing and then there's–"

"The harbor?" Farlan interrupted gently.

"Oh, right. Take the first right past the grocers, it's got the sheep's head over the door, then another right at the church, made of stone that one, then a right after the park, and one last right at the top of the hill and the harbor'll be right there."

Patricia shook her head and muttered.

"That's four right turns."

"Tell your halfbreed to watch her tongue before she loses it. I didn't plan the damn streets, I'm just stuck walking them. You want to take it up with the mayor, you go right ahead. His house is six left turns away."

"Easy, friend," Farlan said soothingly, shooting Patricia a warning glance. "We'll be on our way."

"Just make sure you keep that mongrel of yours under control," the watchman responded, giving Patricia another ugly look. "How you keep your bed warm's up to you, but the powers that be take a dim view of her kind causing trouble."

"I'll keep that in mind," Farlan said genially, nudging Proof towards him. A hoof came down on the watchman's foot, eliciting a series of curses. "Sorry about that. Sometimes she seems to have a mind of her own. Stay safe, friend."

Patricia followed Farlan past the still cursing figure but the watchman was too engrossed in his own pain to pay attention to her anymore. After several seconds, the fog laid its deafening mantle over them once again, and the looming buildings of Fort Eden began their slow slide through the grey. Farlan coughed and reached for his flask.

"Sorry about that, lass. I know you wanted to shoot the bastard but the Cullers have to come first, and we can't risk making waves just yet."

Farlan sounded... tired. Angry. The flask tilted up, then down.

"I told you," Patricia replied, barely keeping the seething

anger from her voice. "They don't care that I'm here to save them. They just see a *mongrel*."

"Aye, and it's not right, and I know you're worth ten of that piece of sheepshit. How many times have you saved my life now?"

"Four, at last count."

"Then you think about that, lass, and not that waste of oxygen back there. You're one of the best of us, Patricia. Don't ever forget that."

"I don't."

Farlan grunted out a laugh and guided Proof past a tall stone church. Oil lanterns flanked its ornately carved front door, the sculpted feet of saints barely visible overhead.

"That must be the church that sheepshit mentioned. Harbor shouldn't be too far."

Patricia eased her hand off her gun and back to her reins, trying to restore some sense of calm. In the distance, the hushed roll of the ocean started to creep into her consciousness, along with the cries of gulls. Lanterns started appearing more frequently, along with men pushing handcarts, the business of Fort Eden's port not slowing even at night.

"Who are we meeting, anyway?"

"An old comrade. You worked with him a couple times before. Luc Barbier."

"The Strategist? You think things are that dire?"

"I'd rather not risk an entire city by being wrong."

A new voice intruded, its owner a dark figure leaning

against a wall so unobtrusively that up until that point he had seemed part of the background. A tri-cornered hat shaded his face. A long barreled rifle rested next to him, and at his feet was a pack bulging at the seams.

"I don't think you are wrong, old friend."

6

A Flock of Falcons

"LUC, YOU FROGGIE BASTARD!" Farlan roared, his weathered face breaking into a broad grin. He dismounted and wrapped the lanky man in a bear hug. "How in God's name are you?"

"Good, Farlan." Luc's voice came out as a strangled wheeze. "Aside from those ribs you're cracking."

Farlan chuckled, gave his fellow Falconer a final squeeze and then released him.

"Hello, Patricia," offered Luc with a small smile as he smoothed his shirt front and straightened his jacket. Patricia inclined her head and gracefully slid from her horse. "It is good to see you both. Now, Farlan, what manner of Culler are we dealing with here? Your telegraph was… ominous."

"That's the problem, Luc. I'm not rightly sure. My nephew's letter didn't mention much more than a local merchant with far less gold in his vault than he should've. He thought it a mite suspicious."

Patricia raised an eyebrow at Farlan. "I never knew you had a nephew in the Falconers. What's his name?"

Farlan ducked his head, an abashed look stealing over his face. "William, and the lad isn't exactly a Falconer."

"Oh? Then how did he know to contact you?"

"Well, you know how it is. You're at a family gathering, the drinks are flowing, pork pies are sitting solid in your belly as you recline next to the fire, and as the night carries on, the stories, well, they're just begging to be told."

Patricia gave Farlan a steely look. "Farlan. We swore an oath of secrecy."

"Aye, lass, that we did, but William is family. I'd trust the lad with my life."

"And it's a good thing he knows about Cullers," Luc interjected, "otherwise we might not have learned about Fort Eden until the corpses started piling up. Based on the relative calm of the town, I think we can assume it's not a Hunter."

"Aye, I didn't think so either," Farlan replied. "Means we're dealing with a Seeder. Damn thing's probably impersonating someone in the bank, and now it's working to get rid of the only thing that'll kill it before it starts whatever trouble it's brewing."

Luc's mouth twisted in a sour smile. "I wish I could argue with that logic, Patricia, but it is true… very well. Farlan, do we have a plan?"

"Aye. We'll ride to William's house and ask him exactly what he saw. With any luck, he can lead us right to the beast. Then you'll figure us out a plan to kill it."

"Hah. Some things never change," Luc said, gathering his

gear. "Where does your nephew live?"

Farlan swung a leg up over Proof, adjusting his leather coat about him to the sound of jostling glass. "Well, ahhh, I'm not quite sure. The blighter forgot to put his address on the letter. I was going to ask someone. Care for a drink?"

"Just like old times, indeed," Luc laughed. "No idea where you're going until you get there. You've been assigned to this city for what, almost ten years now?"

"Thereabouts." Farlan pulled out his flask and took a quick slug. "You sure you don't want a nip? This bloody fog isn't getting any warmer."

Luc shook his head, a small grin still on his face. "I can't believe your liver still works."

Luc pulled out a rolled piece of parchment from the over-stuffed bag and unfolded it, revealing a neatly inked map.

"The last time I was here, I made sure to jot down the local terrain. Most of the constabulary live in the eastern part of the city. Much has probably changed with the construction, but the streets should remain the same."

"That pack of yours always has an answer for everything," Farlan smiled, nudging his horse into a walk.

The three moved between the twisted buildings and streets of Fort Eden, Luc occasionally looking at a folded piece of paper clasped in one hand. The sounds of horseshoes on cobbles rang in muffled echoes, a single pair of leather boots whispering in the spaces like the seconds of some ponderous clock. Around them, the grey shoals of fog continued their ceaseless advance on an occasional glowing torch. After what could have been minutes or hours later, a small stone building rose into solidity in front of the three. Two blue-tinted lanterns flanked its rotting wooden door, and bars covered the few windows dotting its unyielding walls. Luc looked over his shoulder at Farlan and Patricia.

"Right where my maps recorded. Remarkable. Though, perhaps not as remarkable when one considers the average government's propensity for allocating funding to new public services."

"Great," Patricia sniffed, dismounting, "they're where you said they'd be. Let's find Farlan's nephew so we can get in out of this freezing fog."

"You said it, lass," Farlan grunted, clapping her on the back. "Even highland winters are warmer than this bloody place."

"You don't get to complain, old man. I grew up here. You didn't. If I say it's freezing, you just smile and nod."

"As you say, lass," Farlan chuckled, "as you say." He banged a gnarled fist on the door, producing a series of dull thuds. "Hail the guardhouse!"

Several seconds passed, and then the door swung open with an audible creak. The bleary eyes of a watchman peered out.

"H– halt. Who... who goes there at this time of... what bloody time is it, anyway?"

"It's neither late nor early, lad," Farlan boomed. "We're looking for a fellow named William MacCallan."

"William... yeah, I know Will. He lives on Potter's Lane.

Haven't seen him in a couple days. Who're you?"

"I'm his uncle, visiting from bonnie Scotland. Can you help us with some directions?"

The watchman yawned, revealing stained yellow teeth. "It's late. Come back in the morning."

"Sorry, lad, but William's expecting us. Wouldn't do to keep the boy waiting."

"Fine… fine. Take a left at the corner, then go down three streets and take a left, but don't count the alleys, otherwise you'll end up in Northside, and then take another left once you reach the Barking Dog tavern, their mutton pies are the best, then take a left through the park, you'll know it when you see it, and once you're through there, it's an easy two lefts past the tannery and then the third butcher's shop. Will's at the fourth house on the right."

Patricia frowned, her lips moving furiously. Farlan grinned at the watchman.

"So the lad's in the Meat District. A fine place to live, if you don't have a sense of smell. Thanks, and a good night to you."

"Yeah, yeah… just try not to make too much noise, right? Some of us are trying to sleep through bloody night duty."

The door creaked shut, and Farlan started off down the street, Patricia and Luc following behind, Patricia still muttering to herself. Finally, she shook her head, and moved up alongside Luc.

"So, do you have any idea where we're going?"

"Of course. The watchman's directions were quite clear."

"Quite clear? The man told us to go left five times."

"Six times, and yes, that's one of the problems with cities built these days. Everyone's so eager to catch up to the Americans, they forge ahead with each piece and forget how the whole is supposed to fit together."

The three passed another towering stone structure, more ornate carvings stretching up into the hidden night. Patricia shivered, and rubbed her hand on the butt of her pistol.

"I don't like it. It feels like walking through the bones of some Victorian skeleton. How are we supposed to track down a Culler in this maze? The damn thing could be hiding anywhere."

Luc shook his head.

"If Farlan's nephew is correct, and we're up against a Seeder, it won't be far from those involved with gold. Seeders are much smarter than Hunters, though not as deadly in close combat, and it'll know it's vulnerable until it can gain influence over everyone nearby. It'll be a close-quarters encounter, fighting through the Seeder's thralls, but that's what you and the old man are here for."

Patricia bared her teeth. "The tip of the spear, huh? Well, you're right about that, Luc. Find it for us and I promise you, it won't live to see the sunrise."

"Of that I have no doubt, Patricia."

The sudden reek of tanning fluids wrinkled Patricia's nose, mixing unpleasantly with the smell of blood and offal from the butcher shops lining the street, and Farlan turned down a narrow lane, muddy gaps appearing between the cobblestones. He looked around at the cramped houses, each seeming to crowd on top of the next, then nodded once, a confident gesture.

"Smells like the right spot! Hope the boy doesn't mind waking a bit early this morning."

"It smells like a rat crawled into a pig's ass and then they both died," Patricia retorted. "How can anyone stand to live like this?"

"You get used to it after a while," Farlan said over his shoulder, dismounting his horse and leading it further down the lane. "Puts the hairs on your chest."

"I don't need any hairs on my chest, old man."

"It is rather unpleasant," Luc agreed, rummaging in his pack. His hand emerged with a small jar, and he dipped a finger into it, then rubbed it beneath his nose. "Here, try this." He handed it up to Patricia.

Patricia stuck her finger into the waxy substance, then pressed it to her upper lip. Almost immediately, the noxious stench of the Meat District died away, overpowered by a tingling burn.

"What on earth is that, Luc?"

"Essence of menthol. I learned about it from an associate of mine who studies cadavers."

"Do I want to know why he studies dead bodies?"

"There is always something to learn, Patricia," Luc replied, "even from the dead. In fact, in our line of work, death is our wisest teacher."

He followed Farlan down the muddy lane. Patricia swung down from her horse and hurried to catch up to the other two, tying her reins to a nearby post next to Farlan's mare, Proof. The three approached a wooden door, a tarnished brass knocker hanging from its weathered surface. Cracked and glazed windows gazed out at them from either side, their clouded surfaces dark. Farlan reached up to grab it, then paused, his eyes tightening, and backed away from the door.

"Luc."

"I see it, Farlan. Patricia, take point."

Patricia felt the pistol slide into her hand like a natural extension of her body, the handle cool and smooth in her grasp, and pushed past Farlan. Behind her, the sounds of Luc and Farlan readying their weapons registered faintly, but her attention was now on the looming domicile. Approaching the door, she saw what Farlan and Luc had noticed.

A series of gouged claw marks on the wooden frame where the lock would normally lie, broken chunks hastily placed back into their original positions, but now damp and drooping.

Patricia took a deep breath, then leaned into the door with her shoulder, shoving it open, her pistol snapping up to cover the pitch-black interior.

7

Bloody Mess

"FARLAN, THE LAMP."

Seconds later, the light from Farlan's lamp revealed the interior hallway of the house, and Patricia fought to keep the gorge from rising in her throat.

Blood painted the walls in sheets of crimson and body parts adorned nearly every surface. A scene of unimaginable violence now illuminated.

Patricia stepped out into the bedroom, a tiny rectangle barely big enough to fit the threadbare mattress and battered chest of drawers that called it home. She took several deep breaths, trying to steel herself for the return to the entryway, and holstered her pistol. Five long steps later, she stood amongst the horrific entryway scene once more, her heart pounding with rage, her eyes misted with sorrow.

"Any clues, Luc?"

Farlan's voice was subdued and Patricia noticed his fingers trembling around his flask.

"The rips in the flesh here and… here," Luc pointed, "indicate that the body was literally torn apart. There are no mandible marks or lacerations that might indicate the serrated chitin of a Hunter."

"It's not a damned Hunter," Patricia growled. "Hunters don't strike in the middle of a settlement, especially not one the size of Fort Eden. They pick people off from the edges."

"Unless directed to do otherwise by a Seeder," Luc replied, poking a bit more forcefully at the dismembered limb in front of him with a pair of forceps. "But I've never seen a Hunter inflict injuries if this...brutality. They're far more precise, favouring efficiency in energy expenditure."

Patrica could contain her welling rage no longer. "Then what the fuck are we supposed to be looking for, Luc?!"

"I don't know, Patricia!" Luc spun around, his eyes flashing. "Look at the door frame! A Hunter wouldn't even think to replace the wood around the lock. And the desk in the study has been ransacked. This has all the hallmarks of a Seeder attack, but it can't be. Seeders don't kill this way either."

"Oh wonderful, if the 'Strategist' doesn't know what the fuck's going on then–"

"That'll be enough!"

Farlan's guttural bellow silenced Patricia and Luc mid-argument, angry words stopping in their throats.

"That's my nephew and his wife lying here. They deserve better than us bickering over their corpses. He was a good lad." Farlan knelt down, tears gathering in his eyes. "He may not have been a Falconer, but he had the heart for it."

Patricia turned her head away, her cheeks burning. Farlan was right. Even if the evidence was impossible, they still had a duty. Whatever shape the Culler assumed, it had to be stopped. She scanned the scene once more, now almost numb to its atrocious tableau.

Something wasn't right.

"Luc, why's that hand twisted up all tight like that? Like it's making a fist?"

"I would have said rigor mortis, however the consistency of the blood suggests time of death was no more than an hour or two ago. If you examine the fingers… wait a minute…"

Luc's voice trailed off, and he reached down to the partially severed arm trailing away from William's torso. With a grunt, he bent the fingers back, the stiffened muscles giving way reluctantly like toughened ivy. A crumpled piece of paper rested in the palm. Farlan picked it up.

"Reggie Hawthorne… the Black Bull… 387 George Street… moves like a roach…"

Jaw muscles clenched, Farlan nodded.

"A good lad. Patricia. Luc. Follow me. I think there's a man we need to ask some questions."

THE FOG PARTED AROUND THE THREE like a ghostly sea before a ship's prow. Deadened hoofbeats tolled like funeral bells in the freezing night air. Up ahead, a pair of lanterns flanked a ramshackle wooden door, yellow light and muffled laughter issuing from the windows set to either side. A lopsided sign hung over the door featuring the crude drawing of a bull goring a man.

"Is this the place, Farlan?" Luc whispered.

"Aye. The Black Bull Hotel. Not the worst lodgings in the city, but nowhere near the best."

"Very well. If you and Patricia would like to search for Mr. Hawthorne, I intend to scout the perimeter."

"Don't get killed, *Strategist*." Patricia offered a light dusting of sarcasm.

Luc simply smiled. "I will do my best."

Luc disappeared into an alley alongside the dilapidated hotel. Patricia felt her lip curl in a sneer and nudged her horse alongside Farlan.

"Figures. When it might be time for action, he's nowhere to be found."

"Easy, lass. It's been a rough few hours and I know you're upset, but let's remember what we're here for. Luc fights in his own way."

"Well if he can't find whatever this thing is for us, I don't know why we need his help."

"He'll find it, Patricia. There's no one better than Luc at putting pieces together. Now let's see if we can track down this Reggie Hawthorne."

Farlan pulled the door open, revealing a taproom crowded with rough men and painted women, screams and laughter mixing together in raucous symphony. A battered piano in the corner jangled out an upbeat tune played with more enthusiasm than skill, the pianist pausing every fifth bar or so to take a swig from his pint glass. In the leftmost corner, a group of men clustered around a table on which cards and coins exchanged hands with ferocious rapidity, along with angry curses and threats. A sign above the bar proclaimed "Please leave all weapons with the barkeep." Multiple bullet holes dotted its length, and the last several letters were all but obliterated from what looked like the remnants of a shotgun blast.

Patricia sighed and stepped over a sprawled body, snores rising from its owner.

"There's no way this is going to end well. Half these idiots are piss-drunk, and the other half are busy catching up."

"It's fine, lass. Just be ready to give as good as you get. These people respect strength, and naught much else."

Farlan shoved his way through the crowd to the bar, applying his elbows in precision strikes to ribs and kidneys to clear a way, staring down anyone who turned towards him with an angry glower. Patricia followed in his wake, her face hard, adrenaline starting to burn through her veins. Tension filled the air, a hot sensation brought about by proximity and drink, twanging her nerves like an over-taut violin string.

"This place is spoiling for a fight, Farlan," she said, leaning in next to his ear.

"Aye, that it is. Wouldn't be a miner's hostel if it weren't. Try not to shoot anyone if you can help it."

"Not promising anything," Patricia muttered.

Seemed like the Black Bull wasn't making any promises either. A bear of a man loomed in front of Patricia, thick black beard bristling like steel wool.

"Now there's a fine woman in need of some fine lovin'!" he roared, cheeks flushed and ruddy, eyes glazed in alcohol. "Come with me, little lady, and I'll show you why they call me 'The Hammer.'" He placed a large hand on Patricia's shoulder, fingers digging through her woolen jacket.

"Take. Your. Hand. Off. Me." Patricia snarled, her tattoos contracting around her tightened lips. The man leaned closer, the stink of cheap beer wafting along his words.

"Now, now, little lady, no need to be rude. I'm sure your island boys can't pleasure you in the way I ca-yeaaarrrghghhhhhhhhhgfdhnnnghhhh…"

Blubbering, the man collapsed to the ground, clutching at his groin, tears leaking from his eyes. Patricia cracked her knuckles, then kicked him in the head for good measure, the *thonk* of her boot lost beneath the bedlam of the taproom. His eyes rolled back, and Patricia stepped past the limp body, joining Farlan at the bar. She leaned forward onto its gouged and pitted surface to listen in on his conversation with the bartender.

"…Reggie Hawthorne?" The bartender's voice was harried, his hands busy wiping down pint glasses with a rag more dirt than cloth. "Yeah, he came in not much more than an hour ago."

"Any idea where I can find him?" Farlan asked.

The bartender scanned the room, then ducked beneath a thrown pint glass that shattered on the wall behind him in a shower of sparkling shards. Resigned to his lot in life, he dropped the rag, grabbed a broom resting behind the bar and began sweeping up the broken glass without complaint.

"Dunno. It's a busy night."

"What if I make it worth your while?"

Farlan dropped a gold sovereign on top of the bar. It vanished, the bartender's hands never seeming to move off the broom.

"Second table in the corner, next to the window. Emaciated fellow, looks like he hasn't eaten in a fortnight."

"Thanks, friend."

Farlan pushed away from the bar and beckoned Patricia to follow, shoving his way back through the crowd. Patricia trailed in his wake, fingers itching to feel the butt of her gun beneath them. The space around them emptied out, revealing a gaunt man sitting at a rickety wooden table, chair leaned against the wall behind him, muddy boots propped in front. A low-tilted bush ranger's hat shaded his cadaverous face, obscuring his eyes. Thick leather gloves covered his hands, arms crossed over his chest. Despite the packed atmosphere of the taproom, none of the other seats at the table were taken.

"Greetings, friend," Farlan said pleasantly. "Mind if we sit here?"

"Yeah," the man growled. "I do."

Farlan ignored him and swung a chair around, resting his

elbows across its back. Patricia remained standing behind him, eyes scanning the rest of the bar and its patrons.

"We're looking for a fellow by the name of Reggie Hawthorne," Farlan continued. "That you, friend?"

"Fuck off."

"Now that's a shame, Reggie. You don't mind if I call you Reggie, do you?" Farlan pulled a sovereign out of his coat and rolled it across his knuckles. "See, I'm paying good money to find the answers to some questions I have, and I was hoping you could help."

"I'm not interested in your money."

Farlan's eyes tightened.

"I had a feeling you were going to say that. Thanks for your time. Take the coin anyway, for your trouble."

Time itself seemed to slow around Patricia as she watched Farlan flip the coin across the table, light gleaming off the golden disc with each spin. It flew through the air, aimed at the man's face. He seemed to spring upright without going through the intervening motions. The coin bounced off his scrawny belly and he flinched away from it, like an animal avoiding a live coal. Patricia sprang into motion without thought.

Reggie's gloved hands darted down towards his coat but Patricia was already leaping towards him, her pistol flying into her hand. She heard Farlan's voice behind her, barely cutting through the pounding of blood in her ears.

"Take him alive!"

With a snarl, she lifted her finger from the trigger and

brought the butt of her gun whipping down at the crown of Reggie's head, intending to disorient him. She was already anticipating the follow-up strike with her left fist when a grip like iron encircled her descending wrist, grating the bones together in a searing jolt of agony.

"Too slow," Reggie hissed, his gaunt face now nose to nose with hers. Dead-white maggots writhed in the corners of his eyes.

Agog, Patricia watched the world whirl around her like a crazed carnival ride, floor and ceiling swapping places, and then a crashing impact of glass sounded around and through her, cold air replacing the stifling warmth of the taproom, followed by a much harder impact on rough cobblestones. The grating jaggedness of broken bone twisted its way through her right arm and leg, and a deeper, harsher pain exploded in her stomach, acid-etched strands of fire dancing along her nerves. She tried to gather her senses, dislocated *wrongness* coursing through her punctured and battered body, but blackness crept closer into her vision, narrowing the world to a distant tunnel.

I've been... thrown out... window...

Clattering bootheels sounded next to her, then faded into the distance, the roar of a shotgun chasing them. Patricia felt her consciousness slipping away, engulfed in a fog of shock deeper than that cloaking the city. A piercing shriek echoed through the night, and then the darkness closed over her.

8

Shattered Glass and Broken Bones

"…TRICIA. PATRICIA!"

Groaning, Patricia opened her eyes to see Farlan's face hovering over her, his expression twisted with anxiety. Waves of nausea pounded through her head, and then the pain from her broken body re-established itself in her awareness. She vomited into the dirt, a thin mixture of bile and blood.

Farlan produced a small glass vial from his sporran and tilted it towards her lips.

"Drink, lass. Hurry now."

Patricia retched again, then weakly opened her lips and let Farlan pour the contents of the vial into her mouth. The cool liquid slid down her throat, thick and viscous, like oily blood. Seconds later, she screamed, hammer-blows of agony punching through her shattered limbs, bones and internal organs reknitting themselves into their proper configurations in a flood of torment like nothing she'd ever felt before.

Mercifully, the pain receded as quickly as it had come, leaving her white-faced and gasping, cold sweat prickling her skin.

"What… what the bloody hell *was* that, Farlan?"

"The tincture? A right pain in the arse to make, and we're lucky I had it. Otherwise, you'd be bleeding out onto the street and I'd be cursing myself for a fool."

"The Culler?"

Farlan shook his head and took a swig from his flask. "That, I have no idea. I should've told you to kill the damn thing, no matter how badly we needed answers."

Trembling, Patricia pushed herself onto one knee, then unsteadily to her feet.

"Never seen anything like that before. It's not your fault. I was overconfident."

Farlan grinned, but it was a pale imitation of joviality.

"We both were, lass, and that was the only healing vial I had. We'll have to be more cautious going forward. Can you walk?"

Patricia took a couple of halting steps, then nodded. Farlan clapped her on the shoulder, almost driving her to her knees once more.

"Good. It ran off this way, and if I know Luc, he'd have caused it some mischief by now."

Patricia tottered after Farlan, her boots shuffling unevenly on the hardened dirt. Behind them, a crowd piled out of the Black Bull, gawking at the broken glass and bloodstained street, but they were soon left behind in the fog. Silence draped itself across Patricia's ears, her mind racing furiously.

"Farlan."

"Mmhmm?"

"That was something new. It had the reflexes of a Hunter, but the look of a Seeder. And yet, it was no Seeder either. I'm… worried."

"Your lips to God's ears, lass. I've never heard of anything in the records like what we just saw. Let's hope Luc fared better than us."

Patricia fell silent, continuing her shuffling walk. Seconds passed, then minutes, mist-shrouded houses sliding past like grinning skulls, lit only by a few torches that sputtered and spat. A figure materialized out of the gloom, long rifle slung over its shoulder, a motionless body lying before it.

"You still alive?"

"Luc!"

"And Patricia too. Truly, a fortunate night."

Patricia flushed, her head dropping. *Just like him to expect me to fail. Like to see anyone else survive getting tossed twenty feet out a window.*

"It was touch and go for a moment," Farlan replied. "Did you manage to kill the beast?"

Luc smiled, laugh lines wrinkling the corners of his eyes.

"Even better. I caught it."

Patricia felt a twinge of shame and fought to quell it. *It doesn't matter if Luc caught it. All that matters is that it's caught.*

"You're a bloody wonder, Luc!" Farlan roared. "See, Patricia, I told you… Luc fights in his own way."

"Yes, well." Luc waved his hand modestly, "there were only three chokepoints to escape from the hotel, and it was a small matter to lay spike traps along them. Owing to the hour and location, it was unlikely that anyone else would be walking the streets right now."

His expression turned thoughtful.

"Speaking of which, I need to go disarm those other traps before some poor innocent gets a nasty surprise. Farlan, Patricia, if you wouldn't mind keeping an eye on the creature?"

"Consider it done," Farlan grinned.

"Very well, then. I'll be back shortly."

Luc strode off into the mist, rifle swinging over his shoulder. Patricia and Farlan hurried over to the downed figure. As they drew closer, Farlan let loose a low whistle.

"Now that's a fine bloody bear trap."

Patricia nodded in begrudging admiration. Reggie Hawthorne lay squirming on the ground before them, three separate jaws of metal teeth embedded in his right calf and thigh, and two coils of rope pinning his arms to his sides. His eyes rolled wildly in their sockets while specks of white spittle flew from the corners of his mouth. One free leg beat a maddened tattoo on the stones, and unintelligible words flew from his lips, twisting through the air like maggots. Then his body froze, and his eyes locked on to Patricia.

"Lucky girl."

Patricia kicked him squarely in the teeth. Shattered bits of enamel and blood flew onto the dirt with a wet splat. Reggie snarled and snapped at her, jagged tooth stumps gnashing just shy of her foot, blood dripping down his chin. She leaned down next to him.

"That's for throwing me out the window," she said, and then kicked him again in the ribs, her toe landing with a dull crack. Reggie wheezed for air as Farlan came up beside her.

"Easy, lass. We still need to ask him what he knows."

Patricia spat.

"He's a Culler. Ask him whatever you want, just let me know when it's time to feed him a bullet."

Farlan sighed.

"Aye, you've got reason enough to hate them, but we still need to figure out what's going on here, Patricia. This lad isn't acting anything like what we've seen before."

"...I know." Patricia let her hand rest on her pistol and gazed at Reggie. "I know."

Farlan looked around at the still empty streets. "We should get moving as soon as Luc is back. The local constabulary are likely to make their appearance soon. They'll ignore a lot, but this they'll have to answer."

Patricia nodded.

"Makes sense. So, where are we going to take him?"

Farlan opened his mouth to answer, but was interrupted by the shrill tweets of a whistle. He looked around and tensed.

"Blast it all. By the sounds of it, we're not taking him much further than the central gaol."

Patricia glanced down at the still twitching Reggie, and

kicked him once more for good measure. He chattered his teeth at her but she ignored it, listening to the cries as the Fort Eden constabulary closed in.

"The same place you broke me out of?"

Farlan raised his hands in the air as figures with guns and badges materialized out of the gloom.

"That it is, lass. That it is. Hopefully they've got short memories."

9

Bars of Iron and Gold

PATRICIA LOOKED AROUND THE ROOM. Patches of mold covered the corners of the dingy grey stone, and condensation beaded overhead. In front of her and Farlan sat a corpulent man, the bottom half of his uniform obscured by a cheap wooden desk. His fingers tapped an uneven tempo on its cigarette-scarred surface, almost upsetting the towering piles of paperwork scattered across its length. When he spoke, it was with a thick cockney accent.

"So, what, you two are some sort of secret agents? Protecting us all from things that go bump in the night, yeah?"

Patricia kept her head down, not wanting the policeman to notice her. Beside her, Farlan began to speak.

"As I told you, we're Falconers. If you could just summon your chief, Mr…"

"Officer…Nash. You think I'm going to wake the Old Man for this kind of trifling rubbish, yeah? Some silly tale about 'Coilers' and 'Falconers' and la-di-folderol?"

A chubby finger stabbed the desk, making a fleshy thump.

"Stuff and nonsense! No, you two are drunkards, along with your friend in the cell back there, and you'll not sneak past my watch. I think you'll be our guests until morning, and once you've sobered up, we'll talk about what your release is going to cost."

Patricia squeezed her fists tight, her lips going white under the shroud of her hair. Sensing Patricia's tension, Farlan spoke again, his tone jovial.

"It's been a long night, friend, and though your hospitality's been lacking, I'm willing to let bygones be bygones. How about you go fetch the chief and we settle this with him, let you get back to sleep?"

"What's that? You trying to–"

Whatever Officer Nash meant to say never reached Patricia's ears. Instead, the meaty thunk of his head slamming into the desk sounded like a pistol shot, Farlan's hand pinning his face to the wood.

"Listen up, friend," Farlan said in a low tone, muscles in his forearm bulging. "I think we've wasted just about enough time here."

Nash sucked in breath to yell, lips whistling like a tea kettle. Farlan's other hand slammed onto the desk a millimeter from his nose, sending cracks splintering out through the wood, and Nash deflated like a punctured balloon. Farlan leaned in close, piles of paper drifting down like falling snow.

"That's right. That could have been your face. Now, I'm not trying to be unreasonable here, but I really think you should go fetch the chief. Now."

Farlan released Nash who wasted no time in bolting for the door, slamming it open in his haste. Farlan settled back into the officer's chair and took out his flask. Patricia let her hands unclench.

"That's really unfair, you know."

Farlan peered at her over the metal container.

"Oh?"

"I wanted to do that. Why do you always get to have all the fun?"

"Rank hath its privileges, lass. Besides, you would've gutted him, and then we'd be in proper trouble."

"We're in the middle of the gaol. We're already in proper trouble."

Farlan laughed. "Not yet, we're not. Stupid blighters didn't think to take my satchel away. I'll blow out another wall if we–"

A tall man with golden bars across his shoulders strode into the room, his face sour, and Farlan jumped to his feet.

"Ahhh, hello, chief, a pleasure to make your acquaintance. I'm Farlan–"

"I know who you are," the man growled. Two more guards, pistols held at their sides, took up position outside the door. "You're the bastard who blew out my eastern wall thirteen years ago. Took me five months to repair that, and three prisoners escaped." His mouth twisted into a grim smile. "Two of the blighters won't trouble the living no more, that's for certain. Never caught that girl, though…"

Farlan tugged at the collar of his shirt.

"Ahem, yes, well, as you can see, I clearly have an official Falconer's medallion right here, my partner as well," a brief gesture towards Patricia, who tried to bury her face even deeper into her chest, "name engraved on the back, such intricate lettering, wouldn't you agree, and there's a prisoner here we desperately need to question."

"And why," the man began, looking thoughtfully at Patricia, "should I care a single whit for what you want?"

"Because, you see, ahem, the various international treaties between the civilized nations makes it clear that Falconers are to be afforded all assistance necessary no matter what the circumstance, and I believe that–"

"You're the third one," the man interrupted, lips pressed together, pointing a finger at Patricia. "I recognize those tribal markings. Not a prisoner that's been through here that I don't remember."

Patricia looked up at him, her eyes blazing. "And what are you going to do about it?"

The warden rubbed his chin thoughtfully. "Well, I could have you shot. There's only two of you, and quite a lot of us." He leaned against the door frame, eyes steady. "However, I have to ask myself – what could possibly cause a fugitive to return to the site of her imprisonment? What dire need would drive her to take such a risk?"

Patricia's right hand reached for her empty holster and the pistol that had been confiscated upon entry to the gaol.

"I'm no fugitive. You bigoted shitheels refused to listen to me back then because you didn't want to face the truth, and I couldn't afford to rot while there's fighting to be done. I'm a Falconer, now, and if you don't let us–"

"Oooh, threats, and here's me quivering in my boots," the chief interjected. "You'll what? Tear this prison down around my head? Visit the wrath of god upon us all?"

"Try me," Patricia hissed, her fingers flexing like claws.

"Calm down," Farlan whispered.

The chief laughed. "What a charming little savage. Fortunately for you both, I've read the telegrams, and I have no intention of holding up Falconers pursuing their prey, no matter how checkered their past. You're a vicious little bitch, but at least you're human, which is more than can be said for some. Follow me."

The chief stalked out of the room, bootheels striking the floor in a crisp staccato. Farlan shook his head and followed, Patricia scrambling to keep pace. Outside, the dismal grey maze of hallways stretched out in multiple directions.

"Can we trust him?" Patricia whispered, her eyes on the chief's back.

"I don't see that we have much choice, lass," Farlan whispered back. "It looks like he's willing to cooperate, which is more than I'd hoped for coming into this pit. Let's play along for now, at least until we get our weapons back."

"You better be right, old man," she muttered.

Barred cell doors passed on either side, the odd cry for

mercy sounding from some. Patricia felt her gorge rise. The words, filled with liquid consonants, tugged at memories of her childhood.

"Those are my people, Farlan. They don't belong in here."

"Steady. I don't like it either, but we're here for the Culler."

"Easy for you to say. Your skin's the right shade to avoid these cells."

Farlan grimaced, his hand dropping to his coat. "Aye, and don't think I don't realize that. I wish we could do something, but the fact remains, if we spend ourselves on the lesser evil, the greater evil will make our efforts moot." His hand emerged with a flask, and he took a long draw. "Or do you think a Culler's going to discriminate when it comes time for the killing?"

Patricia bit her lip, remaining silent. She knew he was right.

"And that's the rub. We do what we have to now, lass, and maybe later we can do what we wish."

In front of them, the chief paused beside a door, his posture stiff.

"Here's where we've been keeping him. Hasn't been more than an hour, maybe two."

Keys rattled, and the door swung open. The chief gestured them inside.

"Go on, ask your questions. Night's getting late, and I'm looking to get some sleep."

Farlan stepped into the room, Patricia on his heels. She glanced around, and sucked in a whistling breath. Farlan turned back to the door, his eyes on the chief.

"Might be a bit tricky to question a corpse, chief."

The ruptured cadaver of Reggie Hawthorne lay face down on the stone floor. Pale chunks of skull, like a gruesome second mouth, protruded from the back of his head, and a glistening trail of slime crawled up the wall and out the barred window.

"This is not good, Farlan," Patricia whispered, and a chill stole over her heart.

10

Brains and Slime

THE CHIEF BURST INTO THE ROOM, his steel eyes blazing.

"What the bloody hell do you mean, a corpse?" His voice trailed off and he stumbled to a halt next to Farlan. "Christ's flaming arse. What happened to my prisoner?"

"Nothing good, chief," Farlan replied soberly. "Nothing good."

He knelt down next to the late Reggie Hawthorne, ran a finger through the slime trail, then brought it to his nose.

"Hmmm. Patricia. Come take a whiff of this."

Patricia turned from her examination of the window and knelt next to Farlan.

"Smells like…" Patricia shook her head. "Smells different. Not Hunter, nor Seeder."

"Aye, lass," Farlan rumbled, "and not like those beasts up at Seacliff either." He spun back towards the door.

"Chief!"

"Y– yes?"

"Who was Reggie connected with in town? Pimps, night-girls, fences, thieves – anyone at all?"

The chief frowned, his eyes creased in thought.

"There's a Pole we've been trying to pin with something for a while, name of Jacek Polanski. Nasty bit of work. Fingers in all sorts of pies – racketeering, prostitution, even a bit of grand larceny. But he's never the one holding the bag when we track it down. Haven't heard of Reggie's name in association with him, but if anyone's mixed up in the underbelly of Fort Eden, it's Jacek."

His frown deepened.

"Also heard tell of a businessman, queer sort of fellow. Moves strange and talks even stranger. John Ewing. The Ewington 'John Ewing'. He's been flashing gold all over the city the last month or so. Reggie couldn't shut up about him at first. Then he got silent, but it stuck in my mind."

"If he's flashing gold, this John Ewing, he's not a Seeder," Patricia said thoughtfully. "Like most Cullers, Seeders don't like gold."

"A solid theory, Patricia," came a voice from outside the cell. Luc poked his head in and sniffed. "Now that's a messy scene, and not at all the way I left him."

"Who the blazes are you? And who let you into my gaol?" the chief snarled.

"Luc's with us," Farlan replied. "He's a Falconer as well."

"Christ on a crutch, there's three of you wankers in my city? I'd better call the stonemason now and save some time."

"I don't anticipate engaging in any structural remodelling,

sir," Luc said, "but I cannot speak for my Scottish associate here. He tends to take the shortest path between two points."

"Speaking of which, where does this window lead to?" Farlan asked, pulling out a pair of scissors and four small glass tubes.

He knelt down next to the mangled corpse and snipped off several pieces from the gaping crater that was once Reggie's brain, placing them into the tubes. The chief swallowed heavily, and tried not to watch the impromptu dissection.

"It overlooks the southern canal. Not much more than an open sewer, to be honest. Most of the surrounding pipes drain along it down to the harbor."

"Shite. Well, that settles that. There's no way to know where the Culler's gone if it slipped into the sewers. We're back to square one."

"Perhaps not," Luc said. "This businessman, John Ewing… if Reggie was interested in him then it follows we should share that interest. There may be a clue or two there." He looked at the warden. "Do you know where he can be found?"

"There's a house, more a mansion, in the Maori Hill District. Pilkington Street. Man's not likely to appreciate being woken at this hour, though."

"We'll burn that bridge when we come to it," Patricia said, stepping out of the grisly cell. "Sleep's a luxury none of us can afford until we catch this thing."

Farlan nodded.

"Patricia's right. The longer it takes us to track the Culler down, the more lives we risk."

11

A Long Night

FOG CONTINUED TO ROLL ALONG the damp cobblestone streets, a slight brightening of the sky the only hint of a forthcoming dawn. Three figures walked through the murk, senses alert and eyes scanning their surroundings despite their ongoing conversation.

"...and the horses are boarded at the Red Grape Inn. We also have three rooms on the second floor, though I had to twist the innkeeper's arm to make sure they were adjacent."

"Good job, Luc. I'll make sure the chief knows to reach us there if he sees anything suspicious. Patricia, how're you feeling?"

Patricia stifled a jaw-cracking yawn, the adrenaline buzz from earlier fading like the night's gloom.

"Tired. More so than usual."

"Aye, that's the secondary effect of the healing draught. Your body's going to need some solid rest soon to replace what it used. We'll head to the inn after we question Mr. Ewing. It's been a long night."

"Works…" she yawned again. "Works for me. Let's try to avoid anything where I get thrown out a window."

"That's the plan. Luc, you know anything about this Ewing fellow?"

"No more than what the chief told us. Rumor says Ewing made it big in his namesake town and then he came here. Bought a flash house on Maori Hill and has shown a good deal of interest in local businesses. Quite the entrepreneur it seems. Though he does sound somewhat eccentric."

Patricia knew she should care, but the tiredness was starting to seep into her bones. Farlan's response came as if from a distance, and a small part of her wondered why it wasn't her saying the words. The rest of her informed her that she needed sleep. Soon.

"Eccentric? In what way?"

"The chief said Ewing's bought controlling interests in a smithy, a gambling house, and three fisheries, and that he's instructed them to only accept payment in gold. They'll pay paper and silver back but they only take pure metal for services rendered."

"Hmm. Sounds like those crackpot end-of-the-world nutters. Stockpiling gold and weapons so they can fight against the hordes of the apocalypse."

"Farlan, we're stockpiling gold and weapons so we can fight against the hordes of the apocalypse."

"Yeah, but we know about the Cullers, Luc. What's their excuse?"

"That's, well, it's…"

Patricia felt their voices fade away, her focus on the remarkable process taking place in front of her. One of her feet would rise, step forward, and then the other foot would rise, and step forward. She didn't know why they were doing such a thing, only that they must. Slowly, a sound intruded into her speculations.

"Patricia. Patricia! You still with us, lass?"

Her perception swam into focus, Farlan's face peering at her from barely a hand's width away. Cotton seemed to coat her tongue and a heavy warmth lay thick upon her brow. Dimly, she tried to recall why she was standing in the middle of a fog-shrouded street.

"I… yeah… what…"

"Damn. Luc, be ready to carry her if need be. That potion took more out of her than she let on. She's barely conscious."

"Still… ready… fight…"

Farlan patted her on the shoulder.

"Just a little bit longer, Patricia, and then you can rest. See? We're already at Ewing's house. We'll just ask him a couple questions and be on our way."

Patricia felt like she wanted to tell him that she was ready, able to take on any foe, but the words kept jumbling in her mouth, like ball-bearings grinding between her tongue and teeth.

"Fight… Ewing… Cullers…"

"Just questions for now. With all that gold he's handling,

he'd be the daftest Culler we ever tracked down."

Farlan propped one of her arms over his shoulder and knocked on a door that refused to resolve in Patricia's vision. A pause, then it squeaked open, and more words dropped into her numb ears.

"…what?"

"We're here to talk with Mr. Ewing. Official business. It's very important that we speak with him about a case we're pursuing. We have a writ from the Chief Constable."

"…wait here."

The heavy fog draped itself back over her mind. Some time passed.

"…very well. Follow me to the study."

Her feet lurched into motion, following their previous pattern. One foot up. One foot down. One foot up. One foot down. A cushion materialized beneath her, attached to an ornate sofa. Sinking into it felt like luxury unimaginable, the slide to unconsciousness a flea's breath away. Farlan's voice, half dreamt.

"Mr. Ewing?"

A stilted cadence, sliding into her mind on wriggling feet. At the end of a tunnel stood a tall man, his eyes flat as glass, hands cradling his elbows as if he were afraid to let his fingers free. He drew closer in jerking steps.

He scuttles like a crab, Patricia thought woodenly, and with a start, realized she didn't know if she'd said the words out loud.

"We have that distinction, yes. Is there something wrong with your woman friend? Does she require medical assistance?"

"She's fine, just a bit tired. It's been a long night. I'm sure she'd thank you for asking, though. Most don't." A small cough. "I'm Farlan, and this is Luc. We were wondering if you could tell us anything you know about a man named Reggie Hawthorne."

The voice, closer, dry as winter dust.

"Reggie... Hawthorne... yes, we believe this name is familiar. He approached us, not several weeks ago. An alarming creature. We are given to understand that he associated with another person, one even more unsavory than himself. A thief of goods, of dreams."

"Do you know that other person's name?"

A tinge of... something, underneath. Patricia tried to force her thoughts in order, to clarify the oddity, but the pillowy mist of exhaustion billowed forth once more, dragging her deeper into its lightless depths.

"Jacek Polanski, and if you are here, we can only assume he has stolen from you as well."

Pregnant silence, the words crawling through Patricia's fading mind.

"He has diverted shipments of gold from us, for purposes unknown, and we would offer you all assistance in tracking this creature down. We suspect him of ill-intent."

She could fight it no longer. Sleep stole over her on soundless feet.

12

Grey Skies and Black Memories

A BODY, LYING ON THE DIRT FLOOR. In front of her, dark hair spilled out like an inkblot. She reached out with a childish hand, knowing what she would find, what she would always find, what she had found those years before.

"Mama!"

Filmy eyes clouded, the life leeched from her emaciated face eaten by the white man's sickness. Influenza. A crude smear of ash across her forehead, "salvation" from the missionary to their savage flock.

Her perspective shifted. Now she was holding her father's letter opener, its weight heavy in her hands, dull golden blade trembling side to side, loud ringing in her ears like a bell at noon. In front of her, that same missionary, black blood dripping down his chest and staining his tailored robes. Cracked yellow teeth grinned at her, his eyes filled with pus and madness. She stabbed him again, and again, and again, the puncturing thrusts jerking him in marionette twitches, but still he reached for her, closer, closer, closer, the nightmares crawling beneath his skin filling her entire world along with steaming gouts of black blood from his chest…

Patricia jerked awake with a startled shout, her heart pounding.

That bloody dream. Ten years and I still can't get rid of that bloody dream.

She looked around, slowly at first, and then with greater urgency, trying to make sense of the unfamiliar surroundings. A thin, scratchy blanket covered her still clothed body, and muted light flowed through a curtained window, the muffled sounds of passersby echoing through. Her saddlebags lay stacked in a corner next to her boots, while a chipped washbasin covered in fading lilies drooped from the wall across from her, a small pitcher perched on its edge.

Someone knocked at the door.

"Are you okay, miss?"

"…I'm fine."

"Only, it's just I need to clean the room, miss, otherwise Master Harlan will be upset if I don't, and it's nearly mid-morning already…"

I must be at the boarding house. Don't know what she's going to clean, though, there's nothing in here but dust and loneliness.

"Give me a minute."

Patricia pushed herself off the mattress, wincing at the sudden tightness in her shoulders and back, and splashed some water across her face, trying to scrub the remnants of sleep away. After a quick trip to the chamberpot she buckled her gun belt around her waist, checked to make sure the draw on her revolver remained smooth, slid on her boots and opened the door. In the hallway beyond, a thin young woman in a maid's apron stood against the wall holding a small bucket.

"Room's all yours."

"Thank you, miss," the maid replied, bobbing a curtsey. "Oh, the gentleman in the next room over wanted you to visit him when you woke." She pointed to Patricia's right.

"Thanks."

Patricia stepped aside to let the maid pass, and rapped on the next door over. It swung open to reveal Luc hunched over a small table, writing furiously. He looked up as she stepped inside, a smile widening his face.

"Ahh, Patricia, you're awake! Excellent. I'm transcribing all the information we collected last night. Quite an eventful evening."

"That's one hell of an understatement, Luc. Where's Farlan?"

"Out and about, trying to track down that Jacek Polanski character."

Patricia leaned against the wall, racking her still foggy brain.

"Oh, right… that merchant mentioned him, yeah? Ewing?"

"Correct. You fell asleep nearly as soon as he started talking, but Mr. Ewing gave us some credible leads to indicate that Polanski masterminded the gold thefts. We left for the boarding house not soon after – Farlan wanted to make sure you got proper rest."

"Considerate of him, especially after dumping that potion down my throat. What's our plan for today?"

"While Farlan's chasing down Polanski's gang, I thought we should investigate Mr. Ewing's holdings, see if any clues pop up. If this mob boss is actually a Culler, he'll probably have left something behind somewhere."

"Like a body or five?"

"Unfortunately, that's generally the case with Cullers. Based on Mr. Ewing's statements, and the information from the chief constable, we know he owns a gambling house, a smithy, and several fisheries. I planned to start with the gambling house, if you'd like to join me."

"Don't see how I can say no to a morning filled with desperate degenerates and rotting dreams. Where is it?"

Luc dotted the last line on the parchment, then carefully brushed fine sand across to dry the ink. His nimble fingers folded it into thirds, and placed it into one of the many pockets of his overstuffed pack.

"Forth Street. The bellboy gave me directions earlier. First we make a left on Frederick, then a left on Harrow, then a–"

"I'll take your word for it," Patricia interjected, waving her hands in acquiescence.

Luc swung his pack onto his shoulders and laughed.

"I still don't understand how you've lived in this area so long, yet gained no knowledge in navigating one of its largest cities."

"I only visit cities for work, Luc," she replied grimly. "In case you've forgotten, I don't exactly fit the expectations of a 'lady'."

"A fair point. Now come! The fair streets of Fort Eden await, and we have a villain to catch."

As they struck out into those 'fair' streets, Luc's expression grew increasingly glum.

"I don't remember it being quite this... dreary, last time I was here."

Around them, people thronged past, hunched into their coats against a biting wind, the sky above the color of dead fish scales. A gust threatened to lift Luc's hat from his head, and he clamped his hand down to keep it in place.

"When was the last time you were here?" Patricia asked.

"Oh, must have been fifteen years or so, during the summer. The ship I was on stopped for several days to take on fresh supplies before continuing to Singapore. Gave me a chance to stretch my legs, get a feel for the town."

"That explains it. Summer's the only time of year this bloody place gets a peek at the sun. Rest of the time it's like this. What was in Singapore?"

"A Culler. Seeder. Wiped three tin mining villages clean away, like they'd never even existed. Almost three hundred dead when all was said and done. At least, we think that's what the final tally was. The carnage was... excessive, and frankly, there wasn't much left that was identifiable."

"Ouch. That's rough, even for a Seeder."

Luc and Patricia stood to the side to let a horse and cart pass, its wooden wheels clicking over the cobblestones. The driver gazed sullenly at them, then spat on the ground, narrowly missing Patricia. She frowned.

"That's new. Usually they just call me a halfbreed whore. Let's keep moving before I give in to my urge to rearrange his face."

Luc continued on without comment, lips set into a thin line, his pack pulled tight against white-knuckled fingers. It wasn't until another four winding turns later that he spoke again.

"I must confess, I do not see why they hold you in such contempt. True, you may not fit the classical definition of the word 'beauty,' but neither are you homely nor lacking in hygiene."

She sighed.

"It's not my looks, Luc, it's what I represent. My people, well, my mother's people, they're thought to be savages. Brutes. Some would say they shouldn't even be called people. And if I was full-blooded, I would be easy. Another ape walking the streets – that they can deal with."

Patricia paused, memories flooding through her mind. Taunts and slurs from the missionary children, worse from the occasional passing merchant or miner. Spiteful looks of unvarnished hatred. The occasional dead rat left on her pillow, or spoiled fruit thrown from a shadowed alleyway on the rare occasions she visited another town.

"My father… in the village, his kind were considered soulless demons. Rapers of the land, of tradition. As far as I know, he didn't treat my mother poorly the few weeks they were together, but he also didn't stick around. She was a brief distraction between jobs, nothing more. I never even knew his face. I just inherited some shade of his skin."

More memories. Bullying at school the few years she went, pages torn from books and filled with crudely gross drawings. Mud smeared on her face, her clothes, her hair. Withering scorn from teachers, and constant punishment for fighting. The stinging crack of a ruler brought down on bare flesh, the deeper bite of its edge drawing blood.

Patricia forced her fingers to unclench from the grip of her pistol.

"And that's where the problem lies. What I am to them, what they see when they see me. An ape mocking its human betters, wearing clothing no ape should wear, or an outsider who could never be considered family. Nothing pure. Nothing good. Just a filthy mixture of things that shouldn't mix."

She raised her hand to her chin, rubbing her moko, and began pushing the memories back down. It wasn't easy, anger and rage snarling for release, but years of practice had given her plenty of time to tighten her inner demons' leash. Beside her, Luc drew in a soft breath, and turned to face her.

"I can't pretend to know everything of what you experienced, Patricia, but I might know some."

He opened his mouth as if to say more, then placed a hand on her shoulder instead.

"Regardless, we are there for each other now. We are Falconers. And if we cannot choose the family we are given, there is still nothing stopping us from creating the family we desire." Luc hesitated. "Though, I am somewhat reluctant to declare any sort of commonality with a man who thinks alcohol and explosions are the answer to every question."

Patricia cracked a grin and put her hand atop Luc's, feeling his bony knuckles beneath her leather gloves.

"Now now, I'd say those are two of Farlan's more redeeming qualities. Thanks, Luc."

He squeezed once, then lifted his hand from her shoulder, rapping it on a sturdy metal door set into ash smeared stone.

"No thanks necessary, Patricia. We must support each other, lest the Cullers rip us apart."

Patricia felt her lightened mood slip away.

"This is Ewing's gambling house, then?"

The door swung open in response, a giant of a man blocking any view of the interior, two curved knives hooked into his belt sash, two glowering eyes set deep beneath beetling brows. Muscles popped and rolled along his crossed forearms, and a wickedly dancing scar ran nearly the length of his hair-matted chest.

"It is."

13

Breaking and Entering

"WHAT YOU WANT?"

Luc stared impassively at the hulking figure blocking the doorway.

"Is this the Gilded Rose? Owned by Mr. Ewing?"

The bouncer growled, and with a start, Patricia realized it was an actual growl, his bare chest vibrating just like a wolf's.

"Who's asking?"

"Assuming that this is the Gilded Rose, we are working with your employer, Mr. Ewing, to track down some gold shipments of his that have gone missing. We'd like to take a look around the establishment to search for any clues that might aid our investigation."

"Boss didn't say anything about nothing."

Luc frowned.

"Apparently an oversight, but not one we should let delay us. Come, my good man, we're only trying to help. The sooner we can inspect the premises, the more likely we are to apprehend the thief."

"No. Fuck off."

More muscles popped across the already existing muscles, and Patricia sniffed. Casually, she pushed past Luc and stood in front of the giant.

"Look, we need to get in, and you're in our way. I've about reached today's limit for politely restraining myself, so move. Now."

The bouncer sneered, revealing jagged yellow teeth.

"You're a mouthy little mongrel, aren't you, bi–"

Patricia didn't give him the chance to finish his sentence, her foot lashing out into his shin with furious speed. The sound of the bone breaking was like a gunshot, and the bouncer toppled over with a high-pitched scream, clutching at his shattered lower leg. Patricia knelt next to him, pulling one of the curved knives from his belt, and placed the point under his chin. A trickle of blood slid down his neck, and his scream died away, strangled by terror.

"That's better. Let's try this again. We'd like to come in. You'd like to keep your tongue in your mouth, and not have it nailed to your balls. Can we come in?"

"Y– y– yes."

"Yes, what?"

"Y– yes, ma'am."

"Very good. See, Luc, any animal can be trained if you're willing to provide it with the proper incentive."

Luc rolled his eyes and stepped over the bouncer, wrinkling his nose at the puddle spreading from the man's crotch.

"Somehow, I do not think The Gentleman's Horse Fancier Quarterly will be asking you for training techniques anytime soon, Patricia."

"Their loss." Patricia hefted the knife in her hand, and the bouncer's eyes bulged even wider. "Relax," she said softly, "I'm not going to kill you. This, however," she brought the hilt of the knife down on his forehead, knocking him unconscious, "isn't going to feel very good." She let the blade fall to the floor and stood up, wiping dust from her knees.

"Was that totally necessary, Patricia?" Luc asked, looking around the small entrance room.

"Yes. For a variety of reasons."

Patricia scanned the room as well, frowning at the bloodstain running along one wall, and the nicks and scars of bladed weapons marring the cheap woodwork.

"Looks like they see a rough crowd in here. Are you sure Ewing sent along word that we'd be looking around?"

Luc tapped a finger against his thigh.

"He did not say so specifically, but I assumed he would realize it would be an objective of ours. How else are we to prove it was Polanski other than recreating his motives?"

Patricia looked over at Luc, an unpleasant sensation blossoming in her stomach.

"Did he actually say he wanted us to prove it was Polanski? Or did Ewing just point us in his direction and say 'arrest that man'?"

Luc frowned.

"Now that you mention it, Ewing himself did not mention anything other than Polanski. It was the chief who gave us the information on the properties. I confirmed with Ewing that he owned them, but perhaps he didn't understand that they would be involved in the investigation. Odd. He seemed to have an acutely aware mind."

Patricia sighed.

"So then, odds are good that Ewing has no idea we planned on coming here. Great. Well, I'm not apologizing to the bouncer. He had it coming. Guess we might as well look around while we're here." She pushed the door halfway open, then paused. "Oh, and Luc? Next time, when it comes to things like 'getting permission to search a possibly illegal gambling house,' make sure that the conversations you're having with other people aren't just taking place in your head."

A flush stole over Luc's cheeks.

"I will. Sorry."

"It's fine. I can't wait to tell Farlan about 'The Strategist' actually making a mistake."

"Is that really necessary, Patricia?"

"Yes." She grinned. "For a variety of reasons."

The muted clamour of the gambling house washed over Patricia as she walked into the main room, its low-ceilinged length half-filled despite the early hour. Rows of tables lined the walls, occupied by groups of men holding cards and cursing at each other. Large wheels of chance spun lazily, pegs clicking past pointers like rattling bones. A waist-high counter partitioned off the end of the room, heavy iron bars blocking anyone from leaping across it. Behind the bars, several women in low cut dresses sat stoically, faces worn and tired, handing over painted chips and paper money in exchange for the bright flash of gold. Four men toting shotguns leaned casually against the wall behind them, eyes flickering from the transactions to the room and back.

Patricia leaned over to Luc.

"What's the plan? Believe it or not, I'd prefer not to shoot everyone."

Luc snorted, adjusting his tri-corner hat.

"Allow me to attempt a different approach. I anticipate a distinct lack of shooting."

Patricia snorted, but followed Luc over to the counter.

"Well met, madam," Luc began, addressing the hard-worn cashier. "Mr. Ewing, the master of this establishment, sent my partner and I over to ask a few questions about the recent gold heist. Do you have a moment?"

The woman, her painted lashes blinking uncertainly, glanced over at one of the armed men.

"Malcolm. Fellow here says he wants to talk. Says the boss sent him."

Luc waved at the guard strolling over.

"Hello, good sir. Mr. Ewing engaged us at his town house, the one on Pilkington Street. He was quite eager to solve the mystery of his stolen gold. We just need to ask a few questions to anyone who might have been working here on the night of the theft."

The guard frowned, his mouth working as he tried to take in all of Luc's statement.

"…boss sent you?"

"Correct," Luc nodded. "How else would we have entered this fine establishment?"

Patricia carefully looked off into space, thinking of the unconscious bouncer at the front door. Hopefully no one stumbled over him before they left.

"…'k. Be quick, though. Boss don't like it when we're not collecting gold."

"We shall, we shall." Luc turned back to the cashier. "Now then, madam, were you working here a week ago to this night?"

"…yeah. Work every Tuesday. Wednesday through Sunday too."

"Very good. Did you happen to notice anything out of the ordinary, last Tuesday? Anything that stuck in your mind?"

The cashier looked up to the ceiling, her fingers tapping a staccato rhythm on her side of the counter.

"…nah. Things were normal. Gold came in, we made change, wagon came after midnight to collect the metal."

"A wagon?"

"Yeah. Comes every Tuesday. Picks up all the gold, takes it somewhere else. That's all I know."

Luc leaned in closer.

"There's nothing else you remember? Nothing about the wagon itself, maybe the men driving it?"

The cashier's fingers paused, their tapping beat silenced.

"Now that you mention it, yeah. One of the, one of the regulars, had scars all over his hands and forearms. Like little burn marks. Was thinking of asking him for a roll in the hay once he finished work." She giggled. "Always fancied the muscular types, I have. Especially those with thick fingers like him. Oooh, the things a man with thick fingers can do to-"

"Thank you, madam," Luc interrupted hastily. "That tells us everything we need to know. You've been quite a help. Have a pleasant day."

Luc tipped his hat and backed away, pulling Patricia along with him towards the entrance.

"We're leaving already?" Patricia hissed. "We barely looked around."

"We don't need to," Luc whispered back, returning to the foyer and pulling her over the still-unconscious form of the bouncer. "Whatever happened didn't take place here."

"How do you know?"

"The cashier. She described a man with burn marks along his forearms, one of 'the regulars.' What profession tends to pick those up?"

Patricia scowled, the door to the gambling house slamming shut behind her.

"Why don't you tell me and save us some frustration."

"A blacksmith," Luc replied, staring at her intensely. "And who do we know that owns a smithery, along with this palace of ill repute?"

"...Ewing. You think the gold disappeared between here and the smith?"

"It makes sense. Your demonstration to the contrary, one would be ill-advised to assault the guardians of the Gilded Rose, especially if one wanted to make off with large amounts of gold and no one the wiser. Far easier to accost a mere three or four men guarding a wagon traveling across the city, especially if those men lacked awareness."

"So, what, it was an inside job? One of the lackeys at the smith sold out to Polanski for a heist?"

Luc frowned, readjusting his bag straps over his shoulders.

"...could be. Might be something else. We should make the smithery our next stop."

Patricia swung herself up onto her horse, hands unconsciously shifting her pistol into a quick draw position. She clicked her tongue, nudging the animal into a slow walk, Luc keeping pace alongside.

"Makes sense to me. Where's this metal pounder located?"

"Well, first we need to make five right turns..."

14

Farlan's Wrath

"RIGHT, YE BLOODY PILLOCK," Farlan grunted, sweat dotting his brow. "You're gonna tell me where Polanski's at else yer gonna taste my boot by way of yer arse."

With a muttered curse, he twisted the burly dockworker over his hip and slammed him into the rush-covered floor of the squalid tavern, raising a cloud of dust and petrified rat droppings. The few conscious patrons glanced over, then turned back to their cups, bloodshot eyes and tired faces making it clear that unless the building was on fire, nothing would interrupt the serious business of drinking themselves insensible.

Two hulking forms burst out of a back room, nautical tattoos sheathing their arms. They halted at the unmistakable 'snikt' of a shotgun hammer cocking back, barrels like the open eyes of a grave staring down their advance.

"That's right, boyos. This here is between me and yer boss, and he's not worth more attention than one of my hands. Why don't you crawl back over to the bar and buy a round or two.

Courtesy of me."

Farlan spun a golden sovereign at the men and they melted back into the shadows. He grinned, and then turned his attention to the swearing figure trapped beneath his foot.

"Just you and me now, friend." Beneath him, the muscular figure kicked his legs, trying to break free. Farlan lowered the cool metal of his shotgun onto the foreman's cheek, and smiled at the cessation of movement.

"Now now, I'm not asking for much."

"Fuck off, you old bastard. My men are going to break you into dust. If you leave now, we'll pretend this never happened."

"Oh, it's happening all right, and you best wrap your mind around that. Now, all I need is for you to tell me where I can find Jacek Polanski. It shouldn't be that hgnnnnhhhhhh–"

The impact sent Farlan crashing to the floor. Pain radiated up his back and into his skull as the shotgun skittered beneath the bar. Roaring, he surged back to his feet, knuckles clenched into gnarled fists. Across from him, the foreman rose from the floor, his hands in a boxing position, blood trickling down his forehead, three heavyset figures looming behind – the two from earlier flanking an even larger man with one eye. He grimaced and shook out his fingers, his baleful cyclopean gaze locked on Farlan's face.

Farlan grinned savagely, a wild light burning behind his eyes.

"So it's a brawl you want, eh? Fair enough, fair enough. It's been weeks since my last dustup. Don't complain that I didn't offer you the easy way out, though."

With a guttural roar, Farlan launched himself at the right-most longshoreman, his punch descending like a judgement from on high. The man scarcely was able to get his hands up before Farlan's fist slammed into his chin with the force of a thunderbolt. He fell to the floor, insensible, as the other three advanced towards Farlan, hands lashing out like whipping branches in a hurricane gale. But the wily old Falconer dropped beneath their blows and kicked out the knees of the second longshoreman. A swift boot to the chin rendered the man unconscious. Farlan sprang back to his feet, staring down his two remaining opponents.

"Not so confident now, are ye boyo," he laughed, pointing at the foreman's pinched expression. "Seems like your friends might be less conversant in the art of roughhousing than they or you thought."

"Shut yer mouth, old man," the foreman growled, knuckles whitening. "Ain't none of us going to give up Polanski."

"See, you say that now, but you might be whistling a different tune after I loosen a couple teeth. All I want is to talk to him, ask a couple questions."

The foreman spit on the already dirty floor. "And yer ain't getting any answers, copper."

"Do I look like a copper to you, lad?"

Farlan didn't wait for an answer, instead bull-rushing the one-eyed man, driving his shoulder into the other's expansive gut. Air whooshed out of the dock worker's lungs in a sudden gasp and he crashed against a table before sliding down to the floor, limp and wheezing for breath. Farlan turned back to the foreman and presented him with an amiable smirk.

"Now then. Polanski. Where can I find him?"

The foreman gawped at Farlan, his mouth going slack.

"Whu– whu– whu–"

"Come on, now, it was just a tavern brawl. It's not like I–"

At that instant, Farlan realized the foreman's eyes weren't focused on him, but on a point over his left shoulder, and his stomach twisted into a knot. Moving on instinct alone, he dove to the floor, the briefest line of fire tracing itself across the back of his neck. Farlan rolled across the stinking rushes, pushed himself to a knee, and looked over at where he had been just standing. He swore as blood trickled down his spine.

The one-eyed longshoreman had regained his feet, but that wasn't what concerned Farlan. Instead, it was the boiling mass of pitch-dark maggots that had replaced the dock worker's eyeball, and the dull glisten of chitinous claws extending from bloody, ruined fingertips.

"Christ above, that tears it," Farlan muttered. "A bloody Thrall?" He reached down for his shotgun, but his fingers closed only on air. "Bugger."

The Thrall shrieked, a weirdly insectile chittering underlying the explosion of sound, like the clicking of thousands of roach feet beneath an eagle's scream. Behind it, Farlan could see the wooden handle of his gun poking out from underneath the bar, and he swore again. The remaining bar patrons looked up from their drinks once more, then, in unison, drained their cups of their contents and staggered out the door as fast as their limbs could get them there. Across from the Thrall, a dark stain spread down the front of the foreman's pants.

"Whu– whu– what is that th–"

A flashing claw sent the foreman tumbling to the floor. As his crumpled body wept blood in a widening circle, the Thrall hissed and turned towards Farlan, knees tensing into a springing posture. Almost casually, it leaned down and twisted the heads of the two unconscious longshoremen through a full circle, bones snapping with audible cracks. Farlan swallowed heavily.

"Right."

Without seeming to move, the Thrall was in the air, leaping towards Farlan, claws extended. Farlan's hands dipped briefly into his overcoat, then emerged clutching two small vials – one clear, one filled with a viscous silvery liquid. He ducked beneath the lunging strike, ragged talons tearing loose some grey hair with the closeness of their passing, and smashed the silvery vial into the Thrall's chest, then scrambled away next to the bar, putting several metres of distance between them. He then raised the clear vial, as if proposing a toast, as he eyed the silvery mess coating the Thrall's chest.

"I don't suppose you know what happens when sodium and potassium interact with water, do you?" Farlan asked.

The Thrall shrieked and lowered into a charge, claws tearing furrows through the rush covered floor.

"Guess you'll find out."

Farlan threw the vial at the Thrall and then dove over the bar. Almost immediately, a thunderous explosion ripped through the air, along with a continuous popping like water droplets falling into a skillet of hot oil. Waves of heat poured over the bar as Farlan grabbed another flask from his coat and drained it, the familiar burn of whisky sliding down his throat. Hands trembling ever so slightly, he tucked the flask away and grabbed his shotgun, reholstering it. When the popping sound died out, replaced by the more familiar crackling of fire, Farlan levered himself upright and surveyed the damage.

Of the Thrall, not much remained aside from two charred stumps of legs, splintered shin bones poking through blackened flesh, licking flames now consuming even those. Of more immediate concern was the rest of the fire, eagerly feeding on the alcohol-soaked rushes covering the floor. A thin layer of greasy smoke was filling the room.

"Looks like it's time to leave."

He vaulted the bar and made his way towards the door, but stopped on hearing a low moan. Farlan looked around, hearing the moan again, a liquid wheeze coming from the crumpled mess of the foreman. He hurried over to the downed dock-worker and tipped him over to lie on his back, nearly gagging when the ruined mess of the man's abdomen was revealed. Blood welled out from the ragged remains of shredded intestines and lacerated internal organs, and the foreman's face was white and stretched with pain, his chest rising and falling in shallow pants. His lips moved, and Farlan leaned in to catch his words.

"…warn… boss…"

"Shush lad, easy now. Save your strength for getting out of here."

Farlan levered his arms beneath the foreman's armpits, intending to drag him out, but stopped when the man vomited up a rush of bright red blood. More words bubbled up between the hacking coughs of failing lungs.

"…Polanski… warn… monster… French Street…"

Dead weight sagged against Farlan, and with a start, he realized the foreman's chest wasn't moving anymore. Eyes stinging with tears from the smoke, adrenaline and the fury of another life lost to the Cullers, Farlan lay the foreman back down, ignoring the flames rising higher around him.

Finally, he pushed himself to his feet and strode out the tavern's door, the crackle of falling timbers crashing in his wake, the distant clanging of fire alarm bells growing closer in the distance.

15

Springing the Trap

PATRICIA'S HEAD JERKED UP AT the rapping on her door. She rose from the small table where she'd been cleaning her pistol, and moved to answer it.

"Farlan! What happened?"

Dirty streaks of soot smudged his face and clothing, burn marks edged the fringes of his long overcoat. Farlan walked unsteadily into the room, sat on Patricia's bed, and retrieved a flask from his coat before taking a long drink.

"Nothing good, lass. Nothing good. Get Luc. He'll need to hear this too."

"Of course."

Patricia fetched Luc from the adjacent room, and quietly shut the door behind them.

"Ok, we're here, old man. We're here. What's going on?"

Farlan took another swig from his flask, then let out a shuddering breath.

"Had an encounter with a Thrall. At a dockside tavern. It was one of Polanski's men. I killed it, but not before it murdered three others. It was… nasty."

"Gods above," Luc whispered. "Then that means it really is Polanski behind all this. He's the Culler."

"We investigated the gambling house," Patricia interjected. "Had a bit of a scuffle there, but nothing too serious. More importantly, it led us to Ewing's smithery, where we cornered one of the apprentices. He spilled his guts as soon as I pulled out my knife. Polanski was behind the gold heists. The apprentice tipped him off when the shipments were leaving the smithery, and he took care of the rest."

"Good…" Farlan coughed. "Good work, lass. You too, Luc. I got an address from one of Polanski's men at the tavern, before he died. It's a warehouse on French Street."

"In the Devil's Half Acre?" Patricia frowned. "That's a rough spot. Should we see if Ewing can provide us with some extra muscle?"

"Not a bad idea, Patricia, but I think it's best if it's just the three of us," Luc replied. "If Polanski is the Culler, there's no telling how Ewing's men would react when he reveals himself. Far safer to go with less people, but ones you can absolutely rely on, than to have an ally that might get your throat slit."

"Yeah, you're probably right about that. Okay, when are we going to do this?"

"It'll have to be tonight," Farlan said, looking up. "We can't risk Polanski becoming suspicious that four of his men are missing, especially if one was a Thrall. We hit them hard, and we hit them fast, and we let the local constabulary sort out the bodies."

Luc's mouth ticked down.

"I would feel far more comfortable were we to properly reconnoiter the area first. There's no telling what kind of traps the creature might have placed around its lair."

"I wish we could," Farlan responded, "but we have to act now. That Thrall revealed itself in the middle of a tavern. If they're feeling that confident, then there's no time to lose. We have no idea what they're planning, but you both know it won't end well."

Patricia gave a short bark of laughter, the bitter sound echoing through the room.

"That's an understatement if ever I heard one, old man. Nothing involving Cullers *ever* ends well. What's the plan?"

"Well, that's what we need to figure out. Luc, do you still have those maps of the city on you?"

Luc swung his satchel off his shoulder and rummaged through it, emerging with a sheaf of parchment.

"Of course. What were you thinking?"

"The usual. You sneaking and trapping. Patricia kicking in doors and shooting. Me talking to whoever's left."

Luc smiled. "I like this plan."

Patricia nodded her approval. "Me too."

"Good," said Farlan, his own grin gleaming fiercely through the grime on his face. "Because it's the only one we've got."

PATRICIA SHIVERED IN THE COLD MIST of the evening fog and drew her coat more tightly around herself. Her horse whickered, briefly shaking out its mane, then continued its slow walk down the winding street. Gas-lit streetlamps burned fitfully in the gloom, barely illuminating the cobblestones beneath their iron scaffolds. Brief snatches of conversation from workers heading home were swallowed by the heavy air. Soon, it was just her and Farlan, making their way through a shadowed valley of decrepit tenements and slouching warehouses. Next to her, Farlan shifted his weight atop Proof, and pulled out a flask.

"Fancy a drink, lass?"

Patricia bit her tongue on her normal pointed rejoinder, and held out a hand.

"Yes, as a matter of fact. Certain doom really enhances the appeal of liquid courage."

"Well said." Farlan smiled, and handed the flask over. Patricia took a long pull, the fiery whisky burning a path down her throat. She coughed, and handed it back.

"Ugh. Your *waipiro* leaves much to be desired, old man."

"Stinking water, eh? Well, I can't argue with that. I wouldn't waste the good stuff out in the field like this. My ancestors would kill me if I died with a half-full single malt in my coat. No, this is for the effects, not for the flavour."

Patricia rolled her tongue over her teeth, trying to get rid of the metallic aftertaste. Beside her, Farlan took a long drink of his own.

"I damn sure hope the 'effects' get us through the next couple of hours, then. I'd hate to go to the afterlife with that taste being the last I remember."

"We'll make it, Patricia," Farlan replied. "We have to make it. Otherwise the Cullers will wipe out this entire city, and there's no way I'm facing my Granny Agatha, god rest her soul, with that on my conscience."

"You and me both, old man," Patricia muttered, rubbing her hand over her pistol grip. "You and me both."

More fog billowed through the darkness, heavy with the salty brine of the harbour, and other, less redolent scents, its roiling depths cutting visibility even further. Patricia wrinkled her nose.

"Can't see a damn thing, can't smell a damn thing. You sure this is wise, Farlan?"

"Not at all, lass. Still doesn't make it any less necessary. Ahh. We're here."

Warped wooden walls, their painted lengths flaked and peeling like a sunburnt corpse, stretched forth in the small pool of light underneath the hissing gas lamp. A large pair of double doors, a smaller door inset into the right one, split the expanse of rotting timber like palace gates. Farlan dismounted, looping Proof's reins around a hitching post under the lamp, shotgun tucked casually in the crook of his left arm. Patricia followed suit, her pistol held low to her side.

"Now what?"

"We knock, lass, and see if anyone answers. Then we find Polanski and we send that Culler to hell. Luc's waiting on the backside to take out anything that tries to get away."

"Simple enough. I like it. Ready?"

"Ready."

Farlan lifted a hand and banged on the smaller door, sending a series of dull thuds echoing through the night. Patricia cocked her pistol, leaving it concealed by her side, but ready to act on an instant's notice. Adrenaline started its warm surge through her veins.

From the door came a rattling noise, then a creaking groan as it slowly swung open, revealing the dimly-lit interior of a warehouse, boxes and crates stacked in precarious piles, a miniature ramshackle city of sketchy secondhand goods.

"Hello?" Farlan called out.

The doorway remained empty.

"This feels like a trap," Patricia whispered, the back of her neck tingling. She peered into the musty stillness, but nothing revealed itself within the maze of crates. Farlan checked the breech of his shotgun, then snapped it into place.

"Of course it's a trap. Whatever this Culler is, it doesn't seem to be stupid. We're springing it nonetheless."

16

Fiends in High Places

PATRICIA SLID THROUGH THE DOORWAY and knelt behind a mound of crates, her movements fast and sure, presenting a small profile to possible ambushes. The oppressive silence remained unbroken, and she glanced around, trying to take in as much of the interior as she could.

Above her rose a vaulted roof, scarred wooden beams arching across its width, deep shadows pooling within their corners. Underneath them, where the second floor would normally be, a walkway ran around the width of the room, disappearing into a cluster of rooms at the back, hanging like a hornet's nest from the eaves of a house. Lamplight lanced out of two small windows. The light did little more than create darker shadows Patricia's eyes couldn't pierce, and inwardly she cursed.

"Visibility poor. Ambush likely. Moving up, cover me."

"Right behind you."

Patricia edged around the stack of crates, then scurried to a bigger pile, pistol held close to her chest, its barrel pointing unwaveringly forward. She ducked her head out for a quick peek at the rest of the shadowed warehouse floor, then pulled back behind the crates, and looked over at Farlan, who knelt in a firing position by the far wall.

"Nothing over here either. Movi–"

Harsh white light flared from above, and Patricia whirled, her pistol snapping up without conscious thought. On the walkway above stood eleven men armed with rifles, their dark overcoats making them nearly invisible in the deeper shadows of the vaulting beams. A twelfth man in an ill-fitting suit looked down at the two Falconers, a sputtering magnesium torch in his hand casting severe contrasts across his weather-lined face and close-cropped hair.

"Two of Ewing's rats come to sniff around my cheese? What is it that you thought you would find, little vermin?"

"We don't work for Ewing," Farlan called up calmly. "Are you Polanski?"

"So you say, little rat, but you reek of Ewing's type. What possible interest could Polanski find with one such as you?"

"We just want to ask some questions. About anything strange you might have–"

Gunshots split the silence like vengeful thunderbolts.

Patricia flung herself into cover, wooden splinters raining into her hair, her own pistol spitting back thunderous retorts at the assailants overhead.

"Farlan!"

The familiar booming cough of a shotgun answered her, along with a pair of smaller rifle cracks. A brief scream sounded above, followed by a gurgling thump.

"Still alive, lass, though I'll need a fresh pair of skivvies once this is done. Did you see who fired?"

"Couldn't tell. Think they're all Thralls?"

"If they are, this just got a whole lot nastier, and that's the truth."

More gunshots rang out from overhead, and Patricia flinched back down, trying to bury herself into the wreckage of a crate. The smell of coffee rose up around her, and she tried not to sneeze.

Another scream rang out from the walkway, accompanied by a fusillade of shots, and she realized that none of the bullets were hitting near her. Patricia poked her head up to see what was going on.

A strobing nightmare sequence danced on the second floor walkway. One of the men in dark coats, his arms and legs twisted into grotesque proportions, scuttled along the beams of the roof like some hideous spider, finger-talons gouging deep holes into the thick wood, his bare feet elongated to twice their natural length. Two other dark-coated men lay dangling off the railings, their bodies split nearly in half, blood and entrails dripping to the dirty floor below, while their fellows peppered the abomination with gunfire, though it barely seemed to even slow the thing down.

The man in the ill-fitting suit cursed in a string of Polish as he fired a pearl-handled revolver, the magnesium torch in his other hand brandished at the creature like he was presenting a cross to a vampire.

"Farlan! There's a Culler on the ceiling! It's killing Polanski's men!"

Even as she spoke, the Culler launched itself at another one of the men above, absorbing the bullets as its face twisted into a death-rictus smile. Nightmare limbs flashed, twisting the targeted henchman's head clean off with a sickening pop. Blood fountained into the air as the Culler clawed its way back along the ceiling. More bullets followed it, but the creature simply ignored them.

"They don't have any gold, Farlan! We've got to take it down!"

Patricia propped herself up into a kneeling position, and steadied her aim on the edge of a crate, tracking the swift moving Culler's erratic motions across the roof. She drew a breath, held it, then gently let it out as she squeezed the trigger six times. Black blood spurted from the Culler's right shoulder, and it shrieked in rage as it dropped to the floor with a crash. More gunshots rang out from above, chasing the scuttling form into the maze of crates.

"Good shot, lass!"

Patricia pushed herself to her feet and shook her head grimly.

"I only winged it."

"Then let's do something about that. Luc's covering the rear entrance, so if it tries to escape that wa–"

The roar of an explosion rang out from the back of the

warehouse, light piercing painfully through the gloom, and another shriek of rage split the maelstrom of combat. An entire stack of crates slowly toppled over, like an ancient tree falling to the forest floor. Dust filled the air in a hazy cloud, and Patricia quickly reloaded. Another stack of crates, closer this time, pitched over, adding more chaos to the constant rain of gunshots from above.

"It's headed our way, old man! Get your–"

A leaping shape cut Patricia off in mid-sentence, bursting its way through a crate to her right, two outstretched claws reaching for her face. Time itself seemed to slow, her body ever so slightly falling away from the onrushing Culler, and with an icy stab of fear, Patricia realized she wasn't going to get her pistol up in time. Maggots roiled in the ruined mess of its eyes, and its rictus smile stretched even wider, skin cracking and splitting along the sides of its jawline. Ragged black talons filled Patricia's vision, and then her world exploded in a fury of sound and light.

Patricia found herself slumped in the ruined mess of a crate, pistol held limply in her left hand, her right digging a finger into her right ear. Despite her efforts, the ear continued to whine with a shrill, piercing tone. Farlan knelt next to her and pulled out his flask, taking a swig as he stared grimly at the headless corpse sprawled out amongst the wreckage. Black blood steamed in the chill night air.

"Sorry about the tinnitus, lass. Had I any other choice, I wouldn't have fired next to your head."

"Forget it," Patricia replied, her words sounding to her like she was speaking underwater. "I'd rather have a ringing in my head than lose my head entirely. It'll go away eventually."

A pair of boots rounded the corner, and Patricia looked up into Luc's concerned face.

"Are you okay, Patricia?"

"Yeah, Luc. I'm fine. What happened in the back?"

"The Culler dodged the brunt of the nitroglycerin I arrayed across the rear exit, though the detonation was successful in keeping it contained to the warehouse. I did not expect it to move as quickly as it did."

"I don't think any of us expected that," Patricia replied, holstering her pistol and gingerly pushing herself upright. "Speaking of which, we need to talk to Polanski. I know we had him pegged as the Culler, but he seemed just as surprised as we were."

"You aren't wrong, lass," Farlan muttered. "This whole mess feels… off, and I'd like some answers. Luc, is Polanski still here?"

"Yes. Upstairs, with what remains of his crew. I disarmed them, tested them with gold, and told them to sit tight until we could ask them some questions. They seemed inclined to do so. I believe they're in shock at the moment."

"Then we'd best take advantage of that before the constabulary decide to take an interest. Let's go."

17

Unravelling the Shroud

PATRICIA FOLLOWED FARLAN AND LUC UP a rickety wooden staircase to the second floor of the warehouse, the tinnitus still ringing in her ear. Halfway up, the vision of the Culler leaping at her flashed through her mind, its smile a window into the worst hell imaginable. She thrust a hand to the railing to keep herself standing, breath coming in shaking pants. Farlan looked back down at her, concerned.

"You sure you're okay, Patricia?"

"Post battle shakes. I'll be fine. It's just... godammit. It never gets any easier facing those things."

With a wry grin, Farlan waved his flask at her, and Patricia couldn't help but chuckle. After several more deep breaths, the shaking in her legs subsided, and she continued up the stairs, joining Farlan and Luc at the top.

"You have your way, old man. I have mine. The important thing is we keep going."

"True enough, lass, true enough." Farlan turned back to the walkway, then strode forward determinedly to where three men sat slumped against a wall; two in long black overcoats, one in an ill-fitting suit, all with dazed expressions. "Ahh. The very man we were looking for. And how are you feeling, Mr. Polanski?"

The man in the suit looked up at Farlan, some of the fog draining from his eyes.

"What in the blessed virgin's name was that... that thing? Young David was over for dinner at my mother's just two nights ago! How did he turn into... into that *czart*?"

"That, Mr. Polanski, was a Culler, and you are very fortunate indeed to be alive right now, as are your two friends. Speaking of which, who are they?"

"Aron and Borys, both from my hometown in Poland. Good in a fight, not much for thinking. They leave that to me."

"You called the Culler 'young David,'" Luc interjected. "How long have you known him?"

"He... he came to Fort Eden nearly a month ago. He was clever, and not as concerned with the intricacies of property ownership as the constabulary in this city. I tested him, as I do all those who might help me keep this corner of existence alive and flourishing, and he passed, so I allowed him to assist."

"And what did young David 'assist' you with," Farlan asked.

"The smuggling of certain items of high value, some light fencing, an occasional theft. I told you, he was a clever boy."

"When was the last time you saw him? Before tonight?"

"Two nights ago, we have dinner at my mother's. David, he comes because he has no other family here, and family, it is important. This afternoon he shows up to work like normal."

"What about the gold that you stole from Ewing?"

Polanski's face twisted, as if biting into something sour.

"Ewing, that *obesraniec*. He walks into this city like he owns it, starts flashing his money and thinks he can push around those of us who live here, we who look out for the little people. One of my girls, she goes to work at his gambling house, she tells me how much gold he collects, the lower rates he offers to steal my customers. Then one of my dockworkers tells me about fishing ships heading out with heavy crates, many such crates, and coming back with only fish, and these ships bear Ewing's mark. It does not take any genius to put one and two together, so I tell my men we take his gold when he sends it to his ships, and so we did. David, he said we were risking too much, he did not like it, but I tell him that sometimes you must take risks in this line of work, and that also I am the boss and no *pojebany* areshole gets to hide his gold that he steals from me."

Patricia frowned.

"You think he was hiding the gold? Why?"

Polanski shrugged.

"He is *pojebany*. Fucked in head, crazy. Maybe he want to not pay his taxes, maybe he bury it on an island, maybe he worries I will take it back like I did. I do not know."

The three Falconers looked at each other, then Farlan looked back at Polanski.

"Wait here, please. My colleagues and I need to discuss a

few things."

Polanski shrugged again, his face resigned.

"What else is there for me to do? Nearly all my men are dead, and you have the guns to deal with these *czart*, these demons. You have our lives in your hands."

Polanski's head sank down to his chest, his hands limp in his lap, and Farlan motioned Patricia and Luc to join him several metres away.

"I don't like this," Farlan whispered. "His man was a Culler, but I'm not getting any sense that Polanski knew about it."

"I agree," Luc whispered back. "He fits the profile of an immigrant crime lord perfectly, but nothing more."

"So, then what's our explanation?" Patricia hissed. "The missing gold was simply a dispute between two influential men, *and* there happens to be a nest of particularly strange Cullers? That's too coincidental for my liking."

"Mine too, lass, mine too, but it's the explanation that fits. Maybe the Cullers noticed the friction between Ewing and Polanski and simply took advantage of it."

"I agree with Patricia," Luc said, "but I also lack a better means of describing the puzzle we've unearthed than what Farlan offers. It seems that perhaps we got lucky and were able to disrupt whatever it was being planned here before it could ever get going properly. Even the best laid plans of men and Cullers can be disrupted by a chance encounter of fate."

"Whatever was controlling Reggie is still out there," Patricia responded, memories briefly resurfacing.

"Aye, and we'll hunt it down, have no fear about that, lass." Farlan ran a hand through his greying hair. "It seems to me that our best course of action at the moment is to turn Polanski and his crew over to the chief and report what we've found to Ewing. That'll free us from getting entangled in these criminal elements, and allow us to focus on tracking down that last Culler."

"How do you know with certainty it's the last Culler?"

"I don't, Luc, but everything we've encountered has been tied up in the feud between Polanski and Ewing, and whatever that thing was inside Reggie is the only one unaccounted for. Once we track it down, if nothing else pops up, I think we can consider the issue settled."

"That makes sense. Very well, let us alert the local constabulary and then finish our business with Mr. Ewing so I can work on finding the beast. This whole matter has been thoroughly unpleasant, and I would like some respite in order to regain my equanimity."

"We all do, Luc. We all do."

18

Falconer's Heart

THE THREE FIGURES MOVED IN a silent line through the ever thickening fog, lonely islands of humanity in a vast and formless sea. None spoke, each alone with their thoughts from the aftermath of the battle at the warehouse, one taking periodic gulps from his flask. An occasional hissing gas lamp tried to beat back the smothering darkness, but accomplished little more than the briefest moment of lucidity.

Eventually, Patricia nudged her horse alongside Farlan.

"So that's it, then. We saved Fort Eden from the Cullers."

Farlan took another long swig from his flask, unsteady fingers shakily screwing the top back on.

"Aye, lass, we're bloody heroes," he responded sourly, then belched. "Not a damn fool in this entire town will thank us for it, but that's not why we do it, is it?"

"Not at all, but none of this makes sense. What were the Cullers trying to do here? What was their goal?"

Farlan belched again, the acrid reek of alcohol causing Patricia's nose to wrinkle.

"We'll likely never know. Never know why they killed poor William and his wife. Never know what they thought, if they even think. Never know anything except that they kill us, and we need to kill them first. Before they can take everything from us; our lives, our hopes, our families…"

Farlan trailed off, then took another drink, swaying on his saddle, eyes red. The unseen bulk of cramped houses pressed in around them like cilia in some vast gullet, and Patricia pulled her coat tighter around herself, eyeing Farlan's flask.

"Don't you think that's enough for tonight, old man?"

"Bah. What does it matter. Battle's over, and we'll find whatever blew open Reggie's head soon enough. I'll talk with Ewing, let him know he's the new top gangster in town, and then we can finish what's left to finish."

Farlan kicked his heels, causing Proof to nicker, and pulled ahead of Patricia, turning into a faint outline in the fog. She stared at his receding back, then looked over at the sound of footsteps next to her.

"Patricia."

"Luc. I'm worried about the old man. He's hitting that bottle pretty hard."

Luc hitched his pack up around his shoulders and frowned.

"He is, though I cannot say it is out of character for Farlan. He tends towards the maudlin when a mission ends."

"So you've seen him like this before, then?"

"I must confess, never quite this bad, though I've never worked with him on an incident where he lost family. I surmise that it is bringing back memories of his own wife and child, and the drinking is the only way he knows to cope. Perhaps when we track down the final Culler it will bring him some closure."

"I sure hope so. He's not the only one that needs to feel like all this... this death, this waste, whatever fancy word you want to use to describe it, had some meaning."

"Life seldom gives us the answers we desire, Patricia," Luc replied. "We simply do the best we can, and hope that it was good enough."

"But doesn't it eat at you? The not knowing?"

Luc gave her a small, sad smile.

"Of course it does. I, too, wish to know what it is the Cullers want, what motivates them, why they're so inimical to our existence. I want there to be a neat explanation, with a satisfying resolution, all wrapped up in a tidy package, but I've been doing this for a long time, Patricia. Not so long as Farlan, but long enough to know that it's seldom the case. Instead, we muddle through the pain, the fear, the misery, and we take solace in what small salvation we achieve."

Patricia wanted to howl.

"But that's the whole point. How do we know we've accomplished anything? How do we know that we've made a difference?"

Luc waved a hand at the surrounding mist, the muted glow from a window's small candle flickering fitfully overhead.

"We don't, not for certain, but surely these people are safer now than they were before tonight's events? We've rid the city of multiple Thralls and a Culler, and had we not, you know what they eventually do. The destruction they spread. Falconers may be required in Fort Eden again, to protect it once more, but for now, the town has a respite. That has a value inherent in itself."

Luc chuckled grimly.

"Or so I tell myself, when it comes time to lay my head down to rest. If I thought otherwise, it is unlikely I'd wish to continue on with this life."

Patricia found her own lips turning up slightly.

"The great Strategist, showing a heart. I thought we were all pieces on a board for you to move as you pleased. Who'd have thought?"

"I have always had a heart, Patricia, but in our fight against these creatures, to show that invites death. Sometimes a piece must be sacrificed in order to prevail in the game. One day, it might be my turn. One day it might be yours. We must press on, regardless."

"Hopefully that day isn't anytime soon, my friend."

"Am I?" Luc asked softly. "Your friend, that is?"

Patricia found herself in memories once again, the chaos and carnage of the past few days coating everything in shades of red, but Luc always in the right spot at the right time, backing her and Farlan up as if he'd been doing it his entire life.

"Yes, Luc. You are."

"Then that is another success we may attribute to this mission. Look, Farlan has stopped. It appears we have arrived at Mr. Ewing's."

19

Cell Division

FARLAN BANGED ON THE DOOR AGAIN, a staccato sound like clipped gunshots.

"Open up, Ewing. We need to talk."

Seconds passed, then the door swung open, a vaguely familiar man in a butler's uniform standing within. Patricia tried to remember where she had seen him before, then the hazy memories of their first visit surfaced and she realized he was the same servant from their last visit.

"It is late, and the master does not wish to be disturbed. He has had… troubling news."

"Well, wake him up, then. We've figured out what happened to his missing gold. That oughta cheer him up."

"…very well. Please follow me."

The butler motioned them inside, and Patricia followed him and Farlan into the mansion, Luc trailing behind her. An oil lamp cast a dim glow from an intricately carved wooden end table, but did little to brighten the foyer. Patricia scanned the richly furnished room, unable to quite banish the sensation of shadows writhing sinuously in the corners of her vision. Paintings, little more than blotches of color and shape, leered down from the oak paneled walls, and she leaned over to Luc.

"You'd think a rich bugger like him would be able to light his own house," Patricia whispered.

"The rich generally stay rich by not spending their money except when necessary," Luc whispered back.

"Fair enough, but this place gives me the shakes. Feels like we're being watched, but every time I look over, there's nothing there."

"Most likely you're still experiencing adrenaline from our earlier gunfight. Try to relax… Mr. Ewing put us on the trail of the Cullers. We're safe here. And if he wishes to live in the dark, well, the rich don't think like most. Another reason for their wealth, I believe."

"If you say so."

Patricia fell silent as the butler swung open a pair of double doors, revealing a well lit study, tall lamps in each corner casting a warm glow throughout the room, but she couldn't quite shake the sensation of lurking shadows from her mind. A man rose from behind the desk and walked over to them, his movements stilted – the master merchant of Ewington, and now Fort Eden. John Ewing. Another man sat in a chair against the wall, the dark blue of the constabulary neatly fitting his frame, his broad hat tilted low over his face. Recognition dawned in Patricia's mind, but before she could speak, their host stood in front of them.

"We believe we instructed we were not to be disturbed, yes?"

"…apologies, Master Ewing. They said they had news about your gold."

"Very well. Wait outside. We will summon you if necessary."

The butler turned and left, closing the study door behind him with a soft click. Ewing looked at Farlan, tilting his head to the side as if examining a laboratory specimen.

"You have news for us?"

Farlan coughed, and Patricia momentarily feared he would fall over, his body swaying like a ship's mast in high seas.

"Aye, that we do. Oh, hey, it's the chief! That'll save us some time."

Farlan waved at the seated figure, who briefly lifted a hand in acknowledgment, hat still covering his face.

"What's the chief doing here?" Patricia asked.

"A matter that concerns only us," Ewing replied smoothly. "What of the gold?

"We tracked down the cause of the missing shipments. Like you thought, it was Jacek Polanski."

"And you disposed of him?"

"Well, no, that's not what we do. To be perfectly honest, the gold was a secondary concern."

"A… secondary concern?"

"Luc can explain. Do you have anything to drink? I'm parched."

Ewing fluttered a hand towards a sideboard cabinet, and Farlan stalked over, clumsily pulling it open. Patricia frowned.

"We are not actually members of what you would think of as 'traditional law enforcement,'" Luc began, shrugging his pack off and placing it in a corner, along with his rifle. "Instead, we track down creatures called 'Cullers,' and dispose of them via any means necessary."

"...Cullers?"

"Monsters that can sometimes disguise themselves as humans. One variety is a sort of parasitic insect. If left unchecked, they wipe out entire towns, villages, anything they can. We had received news of some irregularities here in Fort Eden, and came here to investigate whether or not there was possibly a Culler infestation."

"And there are many of you doing this?"

"Aye, friend," Farlan answered, gesturing with his nearly full glass. An amber liquid slopped over the side to the carpet below, but neither Farlan nor Ewing seemed to notice. "We Falconers dedicate our lives to rooting out these damn beasts. The bastards kill us wherever and however they can, and if it comes down to them or us, I'm damn well gonna make sure it's us."

"...an entire organisation. We find that... interesting. How do you kill these... Cullers?"

"Gold is the only surefire method we've discovered," Luc replied. "It does something to disrupt their internal chemistry. Hence, our concern when we heard that gold was going missing here – generally, we regard that as a potential sign of Culler infestation. It seems the creatures are aware of their own weakness and act to fortify themselves against it."

Ewing walked over to stand in front of Luc.

"…we understand. Have you discovered anything else about these… creatures?"

"I'm afraid that's–"

"Oh, don't be shy, Luc," Farlan said loudly, his face flushed. "Let the man know. We might need his gold in the future, after all."

Luc pressed his lips together in a thin line, but continued.

"There are two different types of Cullers: Hunters, who tend to act simply and aggressively, essentially killing everything they can, as quickly as they can; and Seeders, who prefer to work from the shadows by sowing fear and confusion with their Thralls."

"Thralls?"

"A lesser form of Culler. Typically an animal of some sort is used as a host, though humans can also be used, and the Seeder controls it via some method that we haven't yet figured out. The Culler does something to mutate its host's body, prioritizing whatever traits give it the most speed and strength, as that's what allows it to cause the most destruction. Thralls are usually twice as strong as a human, Seeders twice as strong as Thralls, and Hunters are pure nightmares to deal with."

"…and those are the only types of Cullers the… Falconers, have discovered?"

"Yes," Luc said, slumping into a chair in exhaustion. "Polanski had multiple Thralls operating within his gang, which we have neutralised. We believe the Seeder was a man called Reggie Hawthorne, though it took a new shape than what we're familiar with. Once we finish tracking it down, Fort Eden should be secure for a time. Any help you can provide with contacts or information would be greatly appreciated."

"...we understand, and will act accordingly. Chief. See to those two."

The warden's head lifted, broad-brimmed hat rising to reveal his face, and the slow surreality of nightmare washed over Patricia. Dead white maggots writhed in the corners of pitch black eyes, and a rictus grin stretched across his face like a jagged tear through flesh. As if in slow motion, she watched Ewing's hand flash through the air in front of Luc, her own hand numbly fumbling at her coat to clear her pistol. Bright red arterial blood sprayed into the air in a sickening fan, and then the chief was in front of her, transfixing her with his now abyssal gaze.

"Too slow, always too slow," he hissed, and a sledgehammer slammed into Patricia's stomach, sending her crashing against the wall in a daze, stars bursting in her vision, her body slamming down into the thick carpet. She heard Farlan roar, and then another crash echoed through the room, the tinkling sound of broken glass mixed in with the dull impact of human flesh against wood. Out of the corner of her eye, she saw the old man lying limp in the wreckage of the sideboard, spirits dripping on and around him.

Groaning, Patricia pushed herself into a sitting position, forcing her unwilling body to cooperate, trying to make sense of the impossible. In front of her, Luc's body slowly fell from his chair, landing in the carpet with a sodden thump, blood weakly pulsing from the gaping ruin of his throat. His eyes flickered, focusing on her, then went glassy and blank. Behind Luc's corpse, Ewing casually flicked blood from ten centimeter long black claws, no expression on his face. Next to her, the door slammed open, the butler bursting through on all fours, arms and legs deformed into sinewy lengths of flesh and chitin, head swiveling from side to side. Saliva dripped from cruelly hooked teeth, and he lunged towards Patricia.

Two percussive bangs shattered her numbness, and Patricia realized she'd finally drawn her pistol, sending the gold-plated bullets ripping into the former butler. Steaming black blood gouted from the cratered mess of his head, body tumbling limply to the floor, and then another sledgehammer blow struck her wrist, the freezing burn of broken bone grating through her nerves. Her pistol flew across the room, and suddenly the warden was crouched before her, hideous smile cracking and splitting the skin of his face.

"Been a while, lucky girl, little girl," he whispered, sibilant words creeping into her ears like spiders. "Last time you put us in a trap, threw us in a cage of stone, made us leave our body, our beautiful, useful body. How lucky for us the master found another."

Casually, he backhanded her, sending her cartwheeling into the corner. More pain radiated through Patricia's neck and body, and she groaned, feeling something sharp digging into her stomach. With her uninjured hand, she felt rough canvas – Luc's backpack – and then the smooth wooden grain of his rifle. She forced her other hand around the stock and clenched the trigger, nearly vomiting with pain.

Please, she thought to herself, *please have kept it loaded.* Her index finger caressed the safety, flicking it back.

Behind her, as if through a distance, she heard the implosive tones of the chief.

"Let me kill her."

A detached, buzzing voice in response, like centipedes stamping out syllables with thousands of tiny feet.

"No. We must learn more about these... Falconers. If they are threats to us, or the other... Elders. Take her body. Tell us what you learn, then use that to infiltrate the others."

"You are the master."

"Yes. We are. Now go."

Footsteps coming closer, the heavy tread of police-issue boots. A presence kneeling down next to her, the cold grasp of a clammy hand. A brief surge of motion, perspective flipping to reveal a leering face, something purple and glistening emerging from a gaping grin. Words crawled out around the obscene protuberance.

"Time to die, lucky girl. Still too sl–"

Patricia swung the rifle under the creature's chin quicker

than thought, her thumb already closing on the trigger. The warden's head disintegrated, black blood spraying through the air above her, hitting the wall with a liquid splat, and she screamed at the pain of the recoil smashing through her broken wrist. Just as quickly, she thrust a knee into the dead Culler's stomach, forcing it off her before blood dripped down and contaminated her flesh, and rolled to her feet, reaching for the rifle with her good hand. Roiling fire raked down the left side of her face, and her vision suddenly narrowed, warm wetness blossoming on her cheek. A weight like a descending star smashed into her chest, and she folded over, coughing liquid chunks of blood and air, the rifle flying out of her hands.

"We knew that one was… brash, but we had use for it. You are trying our patience… Falconer."

Still coughing, Patricia looked up. Ewing stood over her, his once human face now a hideous conglomeration of sharp angles and emerald-faceted eyes, pale skin fading to chitinous black and back again, the mottled hide of a fever dream. Ragged talons flexed and bent at the end of splayed open fingers, and as she watched, a wetly gleaming appendage sprouted from the middle of his face, pulsating veins of flesh extending from the wreckage of what was once a nose. Muscles in his shoulders and back rippled and tore, shredding once finely tailored clothes, and he loomed larger, larger, larger, until it seemed he must brush the ceiling.

"What… what are… you?"

Ewing squatted over her, inches from her face.

"You called us… Cullers, but our kind was old before your kind was a whisper in the primordial night. We have slept for many turnings of this world. You have awoken us."

"I… I don't understand…"

"This world birthed us, gave us life. Gave us meaning, purpose, direction. We defend it from those who would make it uninhabitable for us, as any good children would."

"That… doesn't make… any se–"

Patricia choked at the pressure encircling her neck, Ewing lifting her into the air with one taloned hand. She slapped her hand at the vise-like grip, but might as well have been trying to move a mountain. Blood pounded in her ears, a war rhythm slowly faltering, the half of her vision still left fading to black, the abomination in front of her consuming her sight.

"Your understanding is immaterial. We control the lesser lives. We shall–"

The crystalline chime of shattered glass sounded, and Patricia watched coruscating droplets of amber liquid splatter from Ewing's back and tumble through the air around her, the sharp tang of whiskey stinging her nose. Over the creature's insectile shoulder, she saw Farlan rise from the wreckage of the sideboard, his shirt torn and bloody, golden Falconer medallion swinging above his matted chest hair, a lit match in his hand and fire in his eyes.

"Use yer pendant, lass," he bellowed, and flicked the match at Ewing.

Patricia watched the glacial progress of the tiny burning

stick, uncomprehending, then understanding slammed home like a rifle shot. With a last surge of strength, she reached up to her neck with her good hand, ignoring the iron grip encircling her throat, and fished her Falconer insignia out from beneath her shirt, stabbing it home into Ewing's segmented wrist. A scream like a million angry locusts erupted from the monstrosity, and it let her fall to the floor, spinning to face Farlan. Just then, the match finished its journey, igniting the tattered remnants of alcohol-soaked silks hanging off Ewing's distorted frame.

Flames billowed forth, heat bursting painfully against Patricia's face, and she weakly rolled away from the conflagration, more hideous screams bursting forth from within its roaring depths, the creature stumbling back and forth, setting curtains and furniture alike ablaze. She felt something hard against her knee, sticky wetness soaking through her pants, and looked down to see her pistol, its ivory handle stained red from the pool of Luc's blood. Grimacing, gasping for air, she lifted it in her good hand, its weight like that of the world itself, and sighted down the barrel with her remaining eye.

A demon in bubbling lava filled her vision, its hungry claws reaching for her face, and she squeezed the trigger again, and again, and again, thunderous roars mixing with shrill obscenities born of a throat not meant to contain the words it uttered, until the only sound in the room was the dry click of a metal trigger striking home against an empty barrel and the harsh crackling of flames. Small specks of black crawled forth from the deflating corpse, snapping into the air like fleas on a hot skillet, but none moved after encountering the all encompassing red, their tiny shapes withering beneath the terrible heat.

Patricia's pistol fell from nerveless fingers, thumping against the sodden carpet below, and she followed it into darkness, her last glimpse a pair of boots beneath a kilt rushing towards her.

20

Bottom of the Bottle

FIRE. PAIN. DEATH.

A nightmare of loss and destruction, shadowed tendrils of memory beckoning recollection, fading away into mist under her questioning stare. The crackle of burning wood. The sticky wetness of congealing blood. Scattered remnants of thought, brief glimpses of fog-shrouded houses passing by a bouncing saddle.

Luc.

Patricia burst upright, sleep banished with the surety of a gold-plated round impacting a Culler skull, then groaned in agony. A dull ache radiated from the left side of her face, hot pressure sending its tendrils through her skull. She reached up with her hands, and winced again at the pain from her splinted right wrist.

"Whu... what... hurt..."

"Easy, lass. Easy."

The gruff Scottish burr rolled over her like a balm, a gnarled hand gently pressing her down, and she fell back against the thin comfort of the bedroll.

"Where... are we?"

"The asylum. Seacliff."

Patricia moaned.

"Face... hurts... Luc..."

A deep sigh.

"Aye, lass. He didn't make it, and it's my fault. We're lucky you only lost an eye."

The sound of a fist striking stone. Patricia reached up gingerly to touch her empty orbital socket, vision curiously narrowed, the ache of missing flesh burrowing into her head. Dismal stone surrounded her, dried bloodstains painting two of the walls. Farlan resumed speaking.

"All because I didn't have the damn sense God gave His sheep. I should've known something was wrong. I should've known it was too easy. Instead, I lost myself in the bottle. Didn't see that bastard for what he was."

"Culler...?"

"Dead. You killed it but good, Patricia, and then the house burned down on top of it. I barely got you out in time."

"Luc?"

A heavy sigh.

"Murdered and gone. I couldn't stick around, not with the warden in there as well. No telling what the local boys would've done when they figured out their boss was burnt to ash, with no evidence that he'd been taken by a Culler."

"More... than one, then."

"Aye. No idea what kind Ewing was, but I've never heard of anything like that in the archives." Farlan sat down next to her, his head in his hands. "That was… a nightmare, Patricia, and may God strike me down if I lie. You know I've faced Cullers before, Seeders and Hunters alike, but that… that thing…"

Patricia sat up again, forcing the pain to the back of her mind, thoughts gradually resuming their normal alacrity.

"We need to let the others know. Archivist Llewellyn. The Armourer. Master Woodson."

"I've already sent a message to each. Unfortunately, I wasn't able to obtain any samples, due to dragging you out of the wreckage of that house."

"…not your fault, old man. We all missed it. Even Luc. None of us could have known."

"But *why* didn't we know? Hell, Patricia, Ewing was commanding the others. We've never seen that kind of hierarchical structure in Cullers before, and we've been fighting them for centuries."

Patricia felt unconsciousness beckoning.

"…don't know. Ask the Archivist… or the Master. They're the ones with all the answers."

Her vision narrowed, eyelid drooping over her one remaining eye. As if from a distance, Farlan spoke.

"Aye, lass. We'll get those answers, never you fear. For Luc…"

Patricia slipped back into fitful slumber.

"And for you."

A SHADOWED FIGURE, brown robes draping its body, examined the envelope with a languid gaze, fixating on the postmark. Fort Eden. It flicked a fingernail out, the dull white lengthening to a black sheen of chitin, and slit open the top of the heavy paper, extracting the parchment from within. Several minutes passed, and then it muttered to itself.

"We… are not pleased. This threatens… everything."

Grimacing, it pulled a pair of woollen gloves over its hands, and turned to the fireplace set into the weeping black stones of the fortress. With a quick toss, the message turned to ash, and the figure tucked a golden medallion back under its robe. Light glinted off the swooping falcon before it descended into darkness.

www.ingramcontent.com/pod-product-compliance
Lightning Source LLC
Chambersburg PA
CBHW020731210626
46807CB00016B/1542